HOWLS & HARVEST
EVERSHIFT HAVEN #2
Aurelia Skye

Howls & Harvest

Evershift Haven, Volume 2

Aurelia Skye and Kit Tunstall

Published by Amourisa Press, 2024.

Blurb

I, CANDICE WINTERS, am a big-city event planner, who just volunteered to save Evershift Haven's Thanksgiving festival. I'm not even sure magic exists yet—and I'm already falling hard for a wolfish lycan, who thinks fur is always in season.

I came here from Chicago to visit my sister, Suzette, only to stumble into a town full of magic, quirky residents, and fantastical moments. I've spent my career planning upscale parties and glitzy galas, but when Evershift Haven's Thanksgiving organizer is sidelined by magical morning sickness, I get roped into organizing the town's biggest event of the season. Oh, and my volunteer "partner" happens to be Ronan, a jaw-droppingly handsome lycan—a full-on wolfman, who can't transform to just human or wolf. What you see is always what you get...and I like what I see.

Ronan seems intimidating, but there's gentleness beneath all that fur. He's a big ol' cinnamon roll. I'm starting to see the appeal of magic and small-town life, but I still have one foot in the real world. When Thanksgiving's over, will I return to Chicago? Or will I stick around to make Evershift Haven home?

Welcome back to Evershift Haven—a town that changes itself with the seasons, celebrates every holiday with magical mayhem, and might just inspire you to stay awhile. This second book in the series has all the cozy charm of a crackling fire and pumpkin pie, with a pinch of romance that's as sweet as it is spicy.

Chapter 1

I GRIP THE STEERING wheel of my Toyota, my knuckles white as I navigate the winding Montana road. The GPS on my phone stubbornly refuses to acknowledge the existence of Evershift Haven, but Suzette's directions linger in my mind. "Just follow the feeling," she'd said cryptically over the phone. "You'll know when you're close."

The autumn landscape blurs past my windows in a blur of gold and crimson. I shake my head, still struggling to process Suzette's sudden change in living circumstances. I'm thrilled she quit being an attorney, since it made her miserable and sucked all the fun from her life, but it's a drastic change to uproot everything and move to a small mountain town. Plus, she's been a bit tightlipped about her new life and her boyfriend, Throk.

He's probably some Norwegian guy into Scandinavian death metal with a name like that. Surely, it isn't his given name. I have my doubts and reservations, but Suzette sounds happier than she has in years, so I'm going in with an open mind.

A flicker of movement catches my eye, and I slam on the brakes. There, standing at the side of the road, is Suzette. My sister looks exactly as she always has—perfectly pressed pantsuit, hair neatly pulled back, and not a hint of being a groupie for a death metal band.

"Suzette?" I call out, rolling down my window. "What are you doing out here?"

She strides toward my car with a smile. "Waiting for you, of course. Pull over, Candice. We're almost there."

I obey, guiding my car onto the gravel shoulder. She opens the passenger door and slides in beside me. "Just give it a second," she says, her tone maddeningly calm.

"Give what a second? Suzette, what's going on?"

My words die in my throat as a shimmering flash of light engulfs the car. For a moment, everything goes white, and I squeeze my eyelids shut against the brightness. When I open them again, the world has changed.

Gone is the empty Montana road. Instead, we're parked at the entrance to a quaint town square that looks like it's been plucked from a storybook. Cobblestone streets wind between Tudor-style buildings adorned with strings of twinkling lights. The air is filled with the scent of cinnamon and woodsmoke, and I swear I can hear the faint strains of music drifting on the breeze.

"Welcome to Evershift Haven," Suzette says, grinning at my slack-jawed expression. "Grizelda arranged to bring you straight here. When I accidentally drove through the barrier, it killed Vivi...which reminds me, you're going to love the new her." She grins.

I blink rapidly, certain I must be hallucinating. "This... this isn't possible. How did we get here? Where are we?"

Suzette reaches over and pats my hand. "I know it's a lot to take in. I reacted the same way when I first arrived, but I promise you, everything you see is real...and magical."

I turn to face her, searching for any sign this is an elaborate prank, but all I see is sincerity—and excitement. "You're serious? This place...is actually magical?" I can't hide my skepticism.

She nods. "More than you can imagine."

At her direction, I guide my car through the winding streets of Evershift Haven, my knuckles white on the steering wheel. Suzette chatters excitedly beside me, pointing out various shops and landmarks.

"Oh, look." She gestures to a quaint storefront with a sign that reads "The Whimsical Wardrobe." "That's where I got this amazing sweater that changes color based on my mood. Right now, it would probably be flashing like a disco ball."

I force a laugh, trying to keep my eyes on the road and not on the impossibilities surrounding us. A group of children runs past, one of them floating a few inches off the ground.

"Suzette," I say, my voice strained. "This isn't funny anymore. What's really going on here?"

She turns to me, her expression softening. "I know it's a lot to accept, Candi, but I'm not playing a joke on you. This is real."

I pull the car over, unable to concentrate on driving. "Real? You expect me to believe magic is real? That this whole town is...what? Some kind of magical dimension?"

"Well, yes," Suzette says. "That's exactly what it is. A pocket dimension, where magic thrives and magical beings can live freely."

I close my eyelids, counting to ten. When I open them, the fantastical scene remains unchanged. "Okay, let's say for a moment I believe you. Why are you here? You're not magical."

Suzette shifts in her seat, a hint of excitement in her voice. "Actually, I am. Or at least, I have the potential to be. Remember how I always had a knack for knowing exactly what someone needed in court? Turns out, I have latent empathic abilities. I've been learning to develop them here."

I stare at her, trying to reconcile this information with the sister I've known all my life. "So, you just abandoned your career, your life, for...this?"

"I didn't abandon anything, Candi. I found myself." She reaches out, placing a hand on my arm. "And I think you could too, if you give it a chance."

I shake my head, pulling away. My sister has somehow found herself in a cult. And they use a lot of hallucinogens. That must be it. "This is crazy. We need to leave. Now. You need deprogramming."

"Candice, wait—"

I'm already out of the car, pacing on the sidewalk. A gentle breeze carries the scent of cinnamon and...something else I can't quite identify, along with a faint trace of ozone. Despite my panic, I take deep breaths since the aroma is oddly calming.

Suzette joins me, her expression concerned. "I know this is overwhelming. How about we go to my place and talk? Maybe that will help it feel more real."

I laugh, the sound bordering on hysterical. "More real? Nothing about this is real."

As if to contradict me, a small creature—is that a pixie?—flits past, leaving a trail of sparkling dust in its wake. I watch, mesmerized, as the dust settles on a nearby flowerbed, causing the blooms to grow and change colors.

My sister gently takes my hand. "Come on. Let's start with something simple. Let me show you my home." She takes my hand and leads me back to the car, and I let her.

Once behind the wheel again, I ease my Toyota along the winding road, following Suzette's directions. The trees seem to press in closer, their branches creating dappled shadows on the windshield. As we round a bend, a clearing opens up before us, and I slam on the brakes, my jaw dropping. "Suzette, is that a giant mushroom?"

"Throk's place above the garage was really too small, so Grizelda offered to make us a house." My sister grins. "Welcome to my humble abode."

The cottage before us is indeed crafted from an enormous mushroom, its cap forming a gently sloping roof. Round windows, framed by delicate gills, peek out from the sturdy stem. The entire structure glows with a soft, ethereal light. "This can't be real," I whisper, clutching the steering wheel like I'm about to float away.

"Oh, it's very real," she says, unbuckling her seatbelt. "Come on. I'll give you the grand tour."

I follow her out of the car, my legs shaking. The air here smells different—earthy and sweet, with an underlying tang I can't quite place. When we approach the front door, I notice small jars lining the path, each filled with gently glowing spores. "Are those bioluminescent?" I ask, crouching to examine one more closely.

She laughs. "Something like that. They're fairy lights—literally. Local fairies collect their shed wing dust and store it in these jars. It's a sustainable lighting solution."

I stand up quickly, nearly toppling over. "Fairies? Suzette, what's going on here?" How has my levelheaded sister become...this?

She places a hand on my shoulder, her expression softening. "I know you're in shock, but let's have some tea, and I'll explain everything."

The interior of the mushroom cottage is cozy and warm. The walls curve organically, creating nooks and crannies filled with books, plants, and curious artifacts. A spiral staircase winds up through the center of the main room, disappearing into the cap above.

"This is incredible," I say, running my hand along a smooth, polished section of the inner stem. "How is this even possible?"

She busies herself in the small kitchen area, filling a kettle. "Magic, of course. Evershift Haven isn't just a quirky town. It's a magical community."

I laugh, the sound verging on hysterical. "Magic? Suzette, you're a lawyer, not a wizard. What's really going on here?" My sister has clearly cracked. Or I have.

She turns to face me, her expression serious. "I know it sounds crazy, but I'm telling you the truth. Evershift Haven exists in a pocket dimension, hidden from the rest of the world. It's a sanctuary for magical beings and humans, some with latent magical abilities."

The kettle whistles, and she pours steaming water into two mugs. She hands one to me, and I inhale the familiar scent of chamomile. The normality of the tea is almost jarring in this surreal setting. "So, what? You're saying you're magic now?" I ask, taking a sip of the soothing brew.

She nods, settling into a plush armchair that seems to grow right out of the floor. "I've always had a touch of empathic ability. I could always tell when you were upset, even when you tried to hide it?"

I nod slowly, memories flooding back. Suzette had always been unnaturally perceptive.

"It turns out that was just the tip of the iceberg. When I stumbled into Evershift Haven, I discovered my true potential. I've been learning to harness and develop my abilities ever since."

"But your job? Your life in the city?" I ask, struggling to reconcile this new information with the sister I thought I knew.

Suzette shrugs. "I realized there was more to life than climbing the corporate ladder. Here, I can use my skills to really help people. I mediate disputes between different magical factions and community members right now. It's just a part-time position under Mayor Spellbinder, but it's challenging, fulfilling work."

I shake my head, trying to clear it. "This is insane."

"Look around you, Candi. You're sitting in a house made from an enlarged mushroom. How else would you explain this?"

I open my mouth to argue, but no words come out. How can I argue with what I'm seeing? With what I'm feeling?

A soft chime reverberates through the room, and I jump. Suzette smiles apologetically. "That's just the door. Probably Puckley. She said she'd stop by with some fresh produce."

Before I can ask who Puckley is, the front door swings open on its own. A small, wizened woman with pointed ears and skin the color of tree bark toddles in, carrying a basket overflowing with vibrant fruits and vegetables.

"Afternoon, dearie," she calls out to Suzette. "Brought you some of those singing carrots you like so much, and a few..."

She trails off, noticing me for the first time. Her eyes widen, and she turns to Suzette with a mischievous grin. "Oh, ho. Is this the sister you've told us so much about?"

Suzette nods, standing to take the basket. "Puckley, this is my sister, Candice. Candi, this is Puckley. She runs a magical farm on the outskirts of town."

I stare at Puckley, taking in her otherworldly appearance. "Magical...farm?"

She cackles, and the sound reminds me of wind through autumn leaves. "Oh, yes. Where else would you get singing carrots and mood-changing lettuce?"

I look to Suzette for explanation, but she just shrugs. "Puckley's produce is the best in town. Wait until you try her giggling butternut squash."

Puckley beams at the compliment, then turns her attention back to me. "So, newcomer, what do you think of our little haven?"

I open and close my mouth several times, struggling to find words. "I... it's... I don't know what to think," I finally manage.

The old woman's eyes soften with understanding. "Ah, it's always a shock at first, but you'll see, dearie. Evershift Haven has a way of growing on you."

As if to emphasize her point, a tendril of ivy snakes its way down from the ceiling, curling affectionately around her shoulders. She pats it absently, like one would pet a cat.

"I should be going," she says, heading for the door. "Lots to do before the feast."

With that, she toddles out, leaving me more confused than ever. "Suzette, I think I'm going to need a lot more tea."

Chapter 2

I SIT ON SUZETTE'S cozy couch, my mind reeling from everything I've seen since arriving in Evershift Haven. The quaint town square with its cobblestone streets, the floating decorations, and the unusual residents—it all seems like something out of a fairytale. I'm still not entirely convinced I haven't fallen asleep and dreamed up this whole bizarre scenario.

The sound of a key turning in the lock jolts me from my thoughts.

Suzette, who'd been puttering around in the kitchen, pokes out her head. "That'll be Throk," she says with a smile. "He's just getting home from work."

The door swings open, and I freeze. A massive figure ducks to enter the apartment, and my jaw drops. He's enormous—at least six-five, with broad shoulders and muscles that strain against his T-shirt, but it's not just his size that leaves me speechless. His skin is a deep forest green, with intricate darker green markings swirling across his exposed arms. Small tusks protrude slightly from his lower lip as he smiles. He doesn't look at all Scandinavian.

"Hey, Suz," he calls out, his voice a deep rumble that seems to vibrate through the room. "How was your day?"

She emerges from the kitchen, wiping her hands on a dishtowel. "Pretty good. We've got company—my sister Candice is here."

Throk's amber-eyed gaze locks onto me, and his smile widens. "Ah, Candice. Suzette's told me so much about you. I thought you were coming tomorrow though."

Suzette shakes her head. "I even put it on your calendar." She smacks him lightly on the butt with that admonishment, making his cheeks turn a darker green.

I try to respond, but my voice seems to have abandoned me. All I can do is stare, looking between his green skin, his tusks, and his pointed ears. This has to be an incredibly elaborate costume, right? But as he moves further into the room, the way his skin shifts and the natural way his tusks move as he speaks... It all looks far too real.

"I'm Throk," he says, extending a massive hand toward me. "It's great to finally meet you."

I reach out automatically, finding my hand engulfed by his. His skin is warm and slightly textured but nothing like the latex of a costume. "H-hi," I manage to stammer out. "Nice to meet you too."

He settles into an armchair across from me, the furniture creaking slightly under his weight. "What do you think of Evershift Haven so far? Quite a change from the human world, huh?"

My mind races. Human world? Does that mean... "Are you... I mean, is this..." I struggle to find the right words.

Suzette steps in, perching on the arm of Throk's chair. "Candice, remember how I mentioned that Evershift Haven is a town for magical beings? Throk is an orc."

"An orc," I repeat faintly. "Like from fantasy stories?"

He chuckles. "Those stories got some things right and a lot wrong. We're not the mindless brutes humans often portray us as."

I lean forward, curiosity beginning to override my shock. "So you're really... I mean, this isn't a costume or anything?"

"Nope, one hundred percent genuine orc," he says, flexing an arm playfully. The muscles ripple under his green skin, the tribal-like markings shifting with the movement.

"Wow. I... I don't even know what to say. This is incredible."

Suzette grins. "I know it's a lot to take in. I was pretty overwhelmed when I first discovered all this too. I thought it was a touristy town going way overboard for Halloween. Now, the town has transformed itself for Thanksgiving."

"Town...transformed itself?" I turn to my sister. "And you...you're okay with all this? Dating an orc?"

"Hey, now," he interjects, his tone light but with a hint of steel underneath, "I may be an orc, but I'm still a person. Species doesn't define who we are any more than race does for humans."

My cheeks heat up. "I'm sorry. I didn't mean... This is just all so new to me."

His expression softens. "No offense taken. I understand it's a shock. Most humans don't react nearly as well as you are."

"How did you two meet?" I ask, genuinely curious now that the initial shock is wearing off.

Suzette laughs. "Would you believe his garage was almost the first place I stumbled into when I accidentally crossed into Evershift Haven? My car had broken down—magical interference, apparently—and Throk fixed Vivi for me."

Throk grins, his tusks glinting in the light. "She was so confused." The way he looks at my sister makes my heart melt a little. Despite his intimidating appearance, there's such gentleness in his eyes. He's like a big green teddy bear...er, orc.

"So," I say, resting into the couch. "Tell me more about orcs. Are you all mechanics? Do you have special magical powers?"

Throk laughs. "Not all orcs are mechanics, no. Many of us do have an affinity for working with our hands. As for magic...most beings in Evershift have some magical ability, but it varies widely."

"What can you do?" I ask eagerly.

He shrugs. "Nothing flashy. Sorry. I have an innate sense of how things, particularly machines—magical or mundane—fit together. It's rather common among orcs. Comes in handy in the garage."

"Huh. I can see why you're a mechanic." Part of me marvels that I'm having even a semblance of a normal conversation.

Suzette stands up. "Now that the introductions are out of the way, who's hungry?"

Throk's stomach rumbles. "Oh, I forgot Candice was coming today. Sorry." He nods to me. "Ronan is dropping by some firewood, and I invited him to stay for dinner."

My sister smiles. "The more the merrier." She looks at me. "Why don't you get settled in the loft? It looks like part of the gills in the rafter, but there's an actual room up there."

I nod, still trying to process everything I've seen and heard in the last few hours. "Sure, I'll get settled in." I stand up, wobbling a little. "Loft, you said?"

She points to a ladder tucked against the far wall. "Yep, just climb up there. The room's bigger than it looks from down here." She looks around. "I'll ask Throk to bring in your luggage. I guess we forgot about it."

I nod, thinking my bags were the last thing on my mind earlier. I approach the ladder, eyeing it skeptically. It seems to blend seamlessly with the wooden beams of the ceiling, almost as if it's grown out of the wall itself. I place my hand on the first rung, surprised by its warmth. The wood pulses faintly beneath my palm, almost like a heartbeat.

"Um, Suzette?" I call over my shoulder. "Is this ladder...alive?"

My sister laughs. "Sort of. It's enchanted wood. It won't let you fall."

I inhale and start climbing. As I ascend, the ladder seems to adjust to my movements, the rungs shifting slightly to provide the perfect footholds. When I reach the top, I gasp.

The loft is indeed much larger than it appeared from below. It's a cozy space with slanted ceilings and a large round window that looks out over what seems to be an endless forest. The walls are lined with bookshelves filled with leather-bound tomes, their titles written in scripts I don't recognize. A plush bed sits in one corner, covered in a patchwork quilt that shimmers faintly in the soft light filtering through the window.

"This is amazing," I whisper, running my hand along the spines of the books. One quivers at my touch, and I snatch back my hand.

"Everything okay up there?" she calls.

"Yeah, just adjusting," I say, my voice trembling.

I sink onto the bed, mind whirling. This has to be some kind of elaborate prank or immersive experience, right? Maybe Suzette signed me up for one of those mystery weekends, where you play along with actors in a fictional scenario, but the warmth of the ladder, the subtle movements of the books, the impossible view from the window... it all feels real.

A soft chime echoes through the loft, and I jump. A shimmering image appears in the air before me—a clock face showing it's nearly six p.m.

"Dinner will be ready soon." Suzette's voice floats up from below. "Come on down when you're ready."

I stand up though my legs are still unsteady. "This isn't real," I mutter to myself. "It can't be real." But as I descend the ladder, which once again adjusts to my movements, I find it harder and harder to cling to that belief.

The cottage's warmth seeps into my bones, a comforting presence that feels undeniably magical.

Back in the main room, I find Suzette and Throk setting the table. Throk's massive green hands dwarf the delicate plates he's arranging, yet he handles them with surprising gentleness.

"Feeling more settled?" she asks, glancing up at me.

I shrug, not trusting myself to speak. How can I explain that every moment in this place makes me question my sanity more?

A knock at the door makes me jump. Throk moves to answer it, ducking slightly to fit through the doorway. I stand frozen in place as Throk opens the door, revealing a figure that makes my breath catch in my throat.

The man—if you can call him that—towers in the doorway, his powerful frame barely contained by the entrance. His face is more wolf than human, with a strong muzzle lined with sharp teeth that gleam as he grins. Thick, dark fur covers every visible inch of his body, and his eyes—a piercing, intelligent blue—look at me with an intensity that makes me shiver—with very little fear involved.

"Ronan, come on in, buddy." Throk steps back so he can enter.

The newcomer—Ronan—ducks slightly to enter, his clawed hands gripping a stack of firewood. "Thanks, Throk. Hope I'm not interrupting."

His voice is deep and gravelly, with an animalistic undertone that seems to vibrate through the air. I can't stop staring, gaze darting between his wolfish features, the dense fur covering his arms, and the way his muscles ripple with each movement in that tight flannel shirt.

Throk claps a massive green hand on Ronan's shoulder. "Not at all. We were just about to have dinner, so you aren't late. Ronan, this is Candice, Suzette's sister."

He looks at me again, and I swallow hard.

"Nice to meet you, Candice," he says, setting down the firewood that reveals a thick tail wagging enthusiastically. When he stands up and turns, he extends a clawed hand.

I reach out automatically, and his hand swallows mine. His fur is surprisingly soft, and I feel the strength in his grip. "H-hi," I manage to stammer out. "You have a very...unique look." As soon as the words leave my mouth, I want to kick myself. *Way to go, Candice. Real smooth.*

To my surprise, he doesn't seem offended. Instead, his muzzle curls into an amused smile. "I'll take that as a compliment," he says, a hint of playfulness in his tone. "Not everyone appreciates the rugged charm of a lycan."

"A lycan?" I repeat, my curiosity overriding my embarrassment. "You mean like...a werewolf?"

Ronan chuckles, the sound a low rumble that seems to reverberate through my chest. "Something like that, yeah. Though we prefer 'lycan'—less negative connotations. Plus, werewolves have the ability to shift between human and full wolf form. Lycans are more like the classic wolfman. What you see is what you get," he adds with a little spin.

I can't stop staring at his broad back in the blue flannel, and I suspect he catches me when he completes his turn, and our gazes meet again. Heat suffuses my cheeks. I nod, trying to process this new information. First orcs, now werewolves—or lycans, rather. What's next, vampires?

Suzette emerges from the kitchen, wiping her hands on a dishtowel once again. "Dinner's almost ready. Ronan, you're staying, right?"

"Wouldn't miss it," he says, flashing a toothy grin. "Especially not with new company."

He glances at me again, and the heat returns to my cheeks. There's something undeniably magnetic about him, a raw, primal energy that both intimidates and intrigues me.

"So, Candice," says Ronan as we all move toward the dining area. "What brings you to Evershift Haven? Aside from visiting your sister, of course."

I laugh nervously. "Oh, you know, just thought I'd drop by a magical town full of creatures I thought only existed in stories. Totally normal weekend plans."

Ronan's laugh is rich and warm. "Ah, sarcasm. I like it. You'll fit right in here."

We settle around the table, and I'm seated directly across from Ronan. Suzette brings out a steaming pot of what smells like vegetable soup.

While we begin to eat, I watch Ronan. His table manners are impeccable, despite his clawed hands and elongated muzzle. He catches me staring and winks, causing me to quickly look down at my bowl. Being a vegetarian, I passed on the meaty bones the others have in their soups. I'm not entirely confident those are cow bones, so I probably wouldn't indulge even if I did eat meat.

"So, Ronan," I say, desperate to break the awkward silence. "What do you do here in Evershift Haven? Besides delivering firewood, I mean."

He sets down his spoon, leaning back in his chair. "I'm a lumberjack, actually. My family's been in the business for generations. We supply most of the wood for the town—everything from construction materials to firewood."

I nod, fascinated despite myself. "That must be interesting work. Do you use...magic? Or just good old-fashioned muscle power?"

Ronan flexes an arm playfully, his bicep bulging beneath the flannel. "A bit of both, actually. Lycan strength comes in handy, but we've got some enchanted tools that make the job easier. Plus, it helps to be able to communicate with the forest spirits."

"Forest spirits?" I echo, my eyes widening. "You mean, there are actual spirits in the woods?"

Throk chuckles. "Oh, yeah, the Whispering Woods are full of 'em. Dryads, mostly. They're pretty particular about which trees can be harvested. Some of the trees themselves are magical too."

I shake my head in disbelief. "This is all so incredible. I feel like I've stepped into a fairytale."

He nods. "Trust me, the stories barely scratch the surface of what Evershift Haven is really like. There's magic in every corner of this town."

"Interesting." A little terrifying too.

We continue eating and chatting, and somehow, I'm relaxing more and more. The initial shock of meeting Ronan is wearing off, replaced by a genuine curiosity about him and his life in Evershift Haven. His dry wit and easy charm make conversation flow naturally, and I catch myself laughing at his jokes more often than not.

By the time dessert rolls around—a delicious apple pie Suzette swears was baked by actual fairies—I'm feeling almost comfortable in this surreal setting. Ronan shares tales of his adventures in the Whispering Woods, describing encounters with mischievous sprites and ancient tree spirits.

"There was this one time," he says, leaning in conspiratorially, "When a young dryad decided she wanted to see the town. She literally uprooted herself and started walking down Main Street, trailing dirt and leaves everywhere. Took us hours to convince her to go back to the forest."

I laugh, picturing the scene. "How did you manage it?"

Ronan's eyes twinkle with mischief. "Let's just say, it involved a lot of sweet-talking, a barrel of enchanted sap, and a very reluctant squirrel."

As the evening winds down, I'm disappointed it's coming to an end. Ronan stands, stretching in a way that highlights his powerful physique. "I should get going. Early start tomorrow and all that."

"Right," I say, trying not to sound too eager.

As he says his goodbyes and heads out, I catch myself watching him leave. There's something undeniably captivating about him, a wild energy that both excites and unnerves me.

Suzette nudges me playfully once the door closes behind him. "So, what do you think of Ronan?"

I try to keep my voice neutral. "He seems...nice. Interesting."

My sister laughs. "Uh-huh. 'Interesting.' That's one way to put it."

I roll my eyes but smile. Tomorrow's tour of Evershift Haven suddenly seems a lot more exciting than I had anticipated, and I hope I'll see him again as Suzette shows me around. As I help her clean up from dinner, my mind keeps drifting back to Ronan's piercing blue eyes and that hint of wildness in his smile.

What have I gotten myself into?

Chapter 3

I WAKE UP TO SUNLIGHT streaming through unfamiliar curtains, momentarily disoriented. Then the events of yesterday come rushing back—the magical town, Suzette's revelations, and meeting Throk and Ronan. I sit up, rubbing my eyes. Is this all real or some elaborate dream?

A knock at the door startles me. "Candice? You awake?" asks Suzette.

"Yeah, come in," I say, stifling a yawn.

She enters, already dressed in jeans and a cozy sweater. "Morning, sis. Sleep well?"

I nod. "Surprisingly, yes. Though I'm still not sure if I dreamed everything that happened yesterday."

She laughs. "Trust me, it's all real, and there's plenty more to see. Ready for a proper tour of Evershift Haven?"

"Sounds great," I say, climbing out of bed. "Just give me a few minutes to get ready."

After a quick shower and change of clothes, I join Suzette downstairs. "Thought we'd start with breakfast at 'The Enchanted Espresso.' Their pastries are to die for."

We step outside, and I'm immediately struck by the crisp autumn air and the vibrant colors of the changing leaves. The town seems even more magical in the morning light. Or maybe it's transformed itself even more. I'm starting to believe it can do that.

As we walk, Suzette points out various shops and landmarks. "That's the 'Celestial Clock Tower,'" she says, indicating a tall structure with an ornate face. "At midnight, you can see glimpses of the past or future from the viewing platform."

"Seriously?" I ask, eyes wide.

She nods. "I've only done it once. It's pretty intense."

We arrive at "The Enchanted Espresso," a cozy cafe with twinkling lights strung across the ceiling. The scent of coffee and freshly baked goods fills the air.

"Morning, Bella." Suzette says to the barista, a friendly-looking woman with leaf-red locks. "I like this month's hair color."

"Thanks, Suz—and this must be Candice," she says with a warm smile. "What can I get you ladies?"

"I'll have my usual," says Suzette. "Candice, want to try the Metamorphosis Mocha? It's our specialty."

I hesitate. "What does it do?"

Bella grins. "Nothing too crazy. Just gives you rabbit ears for an hour or two."

"Okay," I say, throwing caution to the wind. "I'll try it."

As we wait for our drinks, I watch in amazement as cups float through the air, gently descending to waiting customers. Our drinks arrive, and I take a cautious sip of my mocha. It's delicious, with hints of chocolate and cinnamon, and a flavor I can't quite place.

"Oh, wow," I say, feeling a tingling sensation spread through my body. I catch my reflection in a nearby mirror and gasp. My usual blonde hair has sprouted bunny ears sticking up out of my thick French braid.

Suzette laughs at my expression. "Looks good on you, sis." She's sporting her own pair of bunny ears.

We grab some pastries to go. "Don't forget, we'll have a new drink starting tomorrow, for Thanksgiving," says Bella on our way out.

Food in hand, we head back out into the town square. While we walk, Suzette tells me more about Evershift Haven's history and the various magical beings who call it home.

"Over there is 'Mystical Motors,'" she says, pointing to a garage where tools seem to be moving on their own. "Throk owns it."

We pass by a park, where the grass seems to be changing colors. "That's Mystic Meadows. The grass responds to the mood of the people in the park."

Continuing our tour, we approach a quaint boutique with a sign that reads "The Whimsical Wardrobe." "This is Madame Threads' place," she says. "She's an incredible seamstress. Her clothes often have magical properties."

We enter the shop accompanied by the sound of a bell tinkling above the door. Racks of colorful clothing line the walls, and I swear I see a scarf slither across a shelf like a snake.

"Suzette, darling." A tall, elegant woman with silver hair glides toward us. "And who is this lovely creature?"

"Madame Threads, this is my sister, Candice," Suzette introduces us. "She's visiting Evershift Haven for the first time."

"Charmed, my dear," says Madame Threads, taking my hand. "Welcome to 'The Whimsical Wardrobe.' Feel free to browse. The mirrors will show you how you'll look in the future wearing any outfit you try on."

As I marvel at this information, the shop door bursts open. A frazzled-looking pale-green woman with wild, silver-streaked purple hair stumbles in.

"Grizelda." Madame Threads exclaims. "Are you all right?"

The woman looks green...um, greener...around the metaphorical gills. "Oh, Threads, it's awful. The morning sickness is back with a vengeance, and my magic is going haywire. I can't keep anything down, and every time I sneeze, something in the house turns into a pumpkin."

Suzette rushes to Grizelda's side, helping her to a nearby chair. "Grizelda, what about the Thanksgiving preparations? Weren't you supposed to start organizing today?"

The green woman groans, putting a hand to her forehead. "I know, but in this condition, I can barely manage to dress myself, let alone plan a town-wide celebration. Oh, what are we going to do?"

I watch this exchange with sympathy for the woman and the town. As an event planner, I could offer at least some assistance, but surely, they wouldn't want an outsider taking over such an important event, would they?

"Candice," says Suzette as she turns in my direction, and her voice is filled with enthusiasm, "You're an event planner. This is perfect."

I blink, caught off-guard. "What's perfect?"

She grins, placing a hand on my shoulder. "You can help organize the Thanksgiving feast. You're the only unattached party available, and your skills are exactly what we need."

My stomach drops. "I... I don't know, Suzette. I'm not even from here. I don't know anything about magical festivals or—"

"Nonsense," interrupts Grizelda, brightening despite her apparent discomfort. "A fresh perspective is exactly what we need, and with your experience in event planning, you'll be a natural."

I glance around the shop, taking in the eager faces of Madame Threads, Grizelda, and my sister. A part of me wants to refuse, to retreat to the safety of the familiar, but another part, a part I thought I'd lost in the grind of corporate events, stirs with excitement at the challenge.

"I... okay," I say, the words tumbling out before I can stop them. "I'll help."

Suzette squeals with delight, pulling me into a hug. "I knew you'd say yes. This is going to be amazing."

Before I can process what I've agreed to, I'm swept out of the shop and into the bustling town square. Grizelda chatters excitedly about the feast's history and traditions, but my mind is spinning too fast to absorb it all.

We arrive at the town hall, a grand building that seems to shimmer and shift when we approach. Inside, a crowd has already gathered. I recognize a few faces from my brief time in Evershift Haven, including Bella from the coffee shop, and Throk, the charming orc mechanic.

As we enter, a hush falls over the room. An elderly man with a long white beard and twinkling eyes steps forward. "Ah, Suzette, and this must be your sister, Candice. Welcome, my dear. I am Ambrosius Spellbinder, the mayor of Evershift Haven."

I nod, suddenly feeling very small and out of place. "Nice to meet you, sir."

He smiles warmly. "I understand you've graciously agreed to help us with our Thanksgiving feast." News travels fast here...supernaturally fast, I guess. "We're most grateful for your assistance."

"I'll do my best," I say, my voice sounding small in the large room.

"Excellent." Ambrosius claps his hands, and a scroll appears out of thin air. "Now, let's go over the details. The feast is in three days, and we have much to prepare."

As Ambrosius begins to outline the various aspects, my event planner instincts kick in. I pull out my notebook and start jotting down ideas and questions. Despite the magical elements, many aspects of planning this feast are familiar.

"We'll need volunteers for various tasks," says Ambrosius, scanning the room. "Ah, Ronan. You'll help, won't you?"

My head snaps up at the name. Ronan, the handsome lycan lumberjack I met yesterday, steps forward. He nods at me, creating a flutter in my stomach.

"Of course, Mayor," says Ronan with a faint growl that's always there. "I'd be happy to help."

Ambrosius beams. "Excellent. You and Candice can work together on the sourcing the ingredients before handling decorations and setup. Caelan will handle the food preparation, of course." He nods to a man with flaming red hair and literal flames in his eyes.

I wonder what kind of creature Caelan is. I swallow hard, suddenly very aware of Ronan's presence. He nods at me with a small smile. "Looking forward to working with you, Candice."

"Likewise," I manage to say, hoping my voice doesn't betray my nerves.

As the meeting continues, I can't stop stealing glances at Ronan. His powerful frame stands out even among the other magical beings, and there's an intensity to his gaze that both unnerves and excites me.

Suzette sidles up to me, a knowing grin on her face as she nudges me with her elbow. "Looks like planning this feast might be more interesting than you thought."

I roll my eyes but can't prevent the smile that spreads across my face. "Oh, hush. We're just working together."

She laughs. "Sure, sure. Just remember, in Evershift Haven, anything is possible."

Leaving the town hall, I'm looking forward to all this with excitement and nervousness. Planning a magical Thanksgiving feast with a handsome lycan lumberjack is certainly not how I expected my visit to Evershift Haven to go, but as I look around at the twinkling lights and the smiling faces of the townspeople, I'm more excited than scared.

LATER THAT AFTERNOON, I meet Ronan in the center of town. "Throk's latest creation. He calls it the Hover-Hauler. Shall we?" He drives us in his strange truck without wheels that mostly seems to drive itself, heading out of the town proper. I roll down the window, and the autumn air carries the scent of ripe apples and freshly turned earth.

"Where exactly are we going?" I ask, clutching my planning notebook in my hand.

He glances at me. "We're visiting some of the local farms to gather ingredients for the Thanksgiving feast. Thought you might like to see where our produce comes from, and the mayor asked..."

I nod, taking in the scenery. The path is lined with trees whose leaves are a riot of reds, oranges, and golds. As we drive, I notice strange, shimmering patterns in the air, like heat waves on a summer day. "What's that?" I point to the distortion.

Ronan follows my gaze. "Ah, that's the magical barrier between farm plots. Keeps the different energies from interfering with each other."

I blink, still not quite used to casual mentions of magic. "Right. Of course."

We approach the first farm, a sprawling field of pumpkins stretching as far as the eye can see. The vines seem to move slightly, even though there's no breeze.

"Welcome to Gourdian's Patch," he says, gesturing to the field. "Best pumpkins in Evershift Haven." He laughs. "You should have seen the chaos last month when Grizelda accidentally enchanted them, and they ran wild."

"Sounds..." I trail off, not sure I want that adventure.

We get out of the truck and walk between the rows of pumpkins. I'm amazed by their unusual sizes and colors. Some are as small as my fist, while others are larger than Ronan. They come in every shade imaginable, from deep purple to shimmering gold.

Out of habit, I lean down to examine a particularly vibrant orange pumpkin. "Aren't you a beauty," I murmur, running my hand over its smooth surface.

"Why, thank you, darling," says a gravelly voice . "You're not so bad yourself."

I jerk back my hand, stumbling and nearly falling. Ronan steadies me with a strong hand on my arm. "Did that pumpkin just...talk?" I ask, squeaking.

Ronan chuckles. "Yep. Gourdian's pumpkins are known for their sass. It's part of what makes them so flavorful."

I stare at the pumpkin, which seems to be vibrating slightly, as if laughing. Cautiously, I bend forward again. "Um, hello. I'm Candice. I'm helping plan the Thanksgiving feast."

The pumpkin's voice softens slightly. "Ah, a newbie. Honey, if you're looking for the best pies, you'll want my cousin over there." A vine points to a plump, pale orange pumpkin a few rows over. "She's got the perfect balance of sweet and spice."

"Thanks," I say, still somewhat dazed. I turn to Ronan. "Is this normal?"

He grins, sharp canines glinting in the sunlight. "For Evershift Haven? Absolutely." We make some selections, and the farmer promises to deliver them in plenty of time for the feast. When we're done, Ronan says, "Let's check out the next farm."

We continue our tour, visiting fields of corn that whisper secrets as we pass, and apple orchards, where the ripest fruit practically leaps into our baskets. At each stop, I'm increasingly fascinated by the magical properties of the produce. I've always loved gardening, but this is something else. So amazing.

In a field of giant sunflowers, I reach out to touch a golden petal. The flower leans into my touch, humming contentedly.

"Oh, my," I say. "They're so alive."

He nods, a soft smile on his face. "Everything here is alive in its own way. That's why we treat the land and its bounty with such respect."

We walk through a patch of enormous, iridescent squash, and I ask, "How does all this magic work with farming? It seems so different from what I'm used to."

Ronan's expression turns thoughtful. "It's a partnership, really. The farmers here use their magic to nurture the land, and in return, the plants share their own kind of magic with us. It's a delicate balance."

I nod, scribbling notes in my book. "And how does this affect the Thanksgiving feast?"

Ronan plucks a shimmering purple squash from a vine before answering. "The magical properties of the produce make for some pretty spectacular dishes. You haven't lived until you've tried Caelan's color-changing pumpkin pie."

I laugh, imagining a slice of pie shifting through a rainbow of colors. "I can't wait to see it all come together."

As the sun begins to set, painting the sky in brilliant hues of pink and orange, Ronan drives back toward town. "We've got one more farm. Puckley's. It's the heart of Evershift Haven's agricultural magic."

I perk up, remembering the small, moss-covered woman I met when I first arrived. "Puckley? The earth sprite?"

He nods. "That's her. Her farm is something special, even by Evershift standards, but," He adds with a wink, "That'll have to wait for tomorrow. It's getting late, and Puckley's farm deserves a fresh start."

I look at him, curiosity burning in my eyes. "What makes it so special?"

His grin widens, showing off his sharp canines. "You'll see. Trust me. It's worth the wait."

As we turn back toward town, I'm filled with anticipation for tomorrow's visit to Puckley's farm, and not just to see how it functions. I'm enjoying spending time with Ronan. Despite my initial skepticism, I'm becoming more and more fascinated by the magic of Evershift Haven. The talking plants, the shimmering barriers, the vibrant colors—it's all so far removed from my usual world of corporate events and spreadsheets.

I glance at Ronan, his powerful form silhouetted against the setting sun. There's something about him, about this place, that makes me feel more alive than I have in years. I'm glad Suzette invited me into this magical world.

Chapter 4

SOFT LIGHT FILTERS through the mushroom house's quaint windows when I wake. The events of yesterday still swirl in my mind like a fantastical dream, but the earthy scent of the room grounds me in this new reality. Magic is real, and I'm smack-dab in the middle of it.

A gentle knock at the door pulls me from my reverie. "Candice? Ronan's here to pick you up," says Suzette.

I hop out of bed, quickly pulling on a flowy bohemian dress and my favorite crystal necklace. As I step outside, he greets me with a smile that makes my toes curl.

"Morning, Candice. Ready for another magical farm tour?" He extends a clawed hand, helping me into the passenger seat.

"You're going to love Puckley's." Ronan slides into the driver's seat, pressing a button on the dashboard. The Hover-Hauler hums to life, gliding smoothly forward. "We're picking up most of the ingredients for the town feast there."

Cruising through town, I marvel at the sights, still not used to all this. Fairies flit between flower baskets, their wings catching the morning light while a group of gnomes argues over the proper way to hang a banner, their voices high-pitched and excitable.

"So, Candice," says Ronan, breaking me from my observations. "What do you think of Evershift Haven now?"

I turn to him, noticing how the sunlight catches the silver streaks in his fur. "It's...overwhelming. Amazing. I keep thinking I'll wake up, and this will all have been a dream."

He nods, his expression understanding. "It's a lot to take in, but you're handling it well. Some humans don't adjust so easily."

"What happens to them?"

He grows serious. "We have ways of erasing memories, if necessary. It's not ideal, but it protects both them and us."

The thought of forgetting all this magic makes my heart ache. "I don't want to forget," I say firmly.

Our gazes meet, and for a second, I'm lost in their piercing blue depths. "I'm glad to hear that," he says softly.

We lapse into comfortable silence as the town gives way to rolling countryside. Fields of shimmering crops stretch as far as the eye can see, punctuated by orchards, where fruit seems to glow with an inner light.

"Here we are," he says as we pull up to a sprawling farmhouse. The building seems to be alive, its wooden walls shifting and creaking as if breathing.

Puckley emerges from the house, her moss-covered skin glowing in the morning sun. "Welcome, welcome." she calls, her voice as rich and earthy as freshly tilled soil. "Come to collect some of the harvest, have you?"

When we climb out of the truck, I'm struck by the vibrant energy emanating from the farm. The very air seems to hum with life. "Puckley," I say, unable to contain my curiosity, "How does magical farming work? Is it very different from regular farming?"

She beckons us to follow her into the fields. "Oh, my dear, you're in for a treat. Magical farming is a dance with nature itself."

While walking, Puckley explains the intricacies of her craft. "Regular farming is all about coaxing what nature has already given—careful timing, feeding, weeding, and hoping the rain falls just right. In magical farming, you're more than a caretaker. You're a partner in the life cycle."

She stops by a row of tomatoes, their leaves shimmering faintly under the autumn sun. "These beauties here have minds of their own—plants know what they need, and they'll tell you, if you're open to listening." She taps her ear, winking at me. "See, enchanted plants like to have a say. They'll grow faster or slower depending on their mood, and the energy around them, and sometimes, they even prefer certain songs over others. You don't just feed the soil. You nourish the spirit of the plant."

I watch in awe as Puckley hums a soft melody. The tomato plants seem to sway in response, their fruits plumping before my eyes.

"That's incredible," I say, "But how do you know what they need?"

She chuckles, digging a hand into a pouch at her waist. "It's all about intention and connection. Watch this."

She sprinkles a pinch of glittering soil around the base of a towering sunflower. The plant shivers, and suddenly, its petals burst into a brilliant array of colors.

"Regular soil, you test it, amend it, do what you must to get the right mix. This here," she says, patting the dirt affectionately, "Is truly living soil. It carries intention. One sprinkle of enchanted soil like this can revive a field or bring strength to a sapling, but it's also sensitive to balance. Too much magic, and you'll get an overgrown forest overnight."

Continuing through the fields, I'm struck by the harmony between Puckley and her crops. Plants seem to reach out to her as she passes, and she greets each one like an old friend.

"What about pests?" I ask, remembering the constant battle against insects and diseases in my small herb garden back home.

She grins, a mischievous twinkle in her eye. "Ah, now that's where it gets fun. In magical farming, we don't fight pests. We negotiate with them."

She leads us to a patch of what looks like ordinary lettuce. When we approach, I notice tiny, shimmering creatures flitting between the leaves.

"These are leaf sprites," she says. "They help keep the plants healthy in exchange for a small portion of the harvest. It's all about balance and mutual respect."

I crouch down, watching the sprites at work. One notices me and zips over, hovering inches from my nose. Its tiny face scrunches up in curiosity before it darts away, leaving a trail of sparkling dust. "They're beautiful."

"Very," says Ronan, his voice soft. I look up to find him watching me, a warm smile on his face.

While we continue our tour, Puckley shares more magical farming secrets. She shows us self-watering melons that store rainwater in pocket dimensions, and pumpkins that change flavor based on the stories told to them as they grow. "And don't get me started on weeds," she says with a laugh. "Pulling them out of regular soil is work, but enchanted weeds? They'll argue with you the whole time, swearing they have just as much right to be there as the crops."

As if on cue, a patch of dandelions near our feet begins to rustle. "We're not weeds, we're wildflowers," says a tiny, indignant voice. "You're just biased against yellow."

"Oh, hush," says Puckley, but kindly. "Dandelions aren't weeds. You have all sorts of culinary, magical, and medicinal benefits." The patch of dandelions preen under her words.

I laugh, delighted by the sheer wonder of it all. "This is amazing. I've never seen anything like it."

Puckley beams at me. "You've got a good eye for it, Candice. I can see the spark of magic in you. Have you ever considered trying your hand at farming?"

The question catches me off guard. "Me? I've thought about it, but it's just a pipe dream. I mean, I have a small herb garden at home, but nothing like this."

"Sometimes, the seed of magic takes root in the most unexpected places," she says cryptically.

Returning to the farmhouse a while later with arms full of produce for the town feast, a sense of excitement bubbles inside me. Ronan helps me load the last of the harvest into the Hover-Hauler. "What did you think of magical farming?"

I look out over Puckley's fields, watching the plants sway in a breeze I can't feel, their leaves whispering secrets to each other. "I think," I say slowly, "I might have found something truly special here in Evershift Haven." Glancing back at him, it's not just the farm that I'm referencing.

Ronan's smile is warm and genuine. "I think you might be right about that, Candice."

A COUPLE OF DAYS LATER, I wake up to the bustling sounds of Evershift Haven preparing for the town feast. The air is crisp with autumn, carrying the scent of cinnamon and woodsmoke. I slip on a flowing skirt and my favorite crystal necklace before heading out to help with the preparations.

The town square is a flurry of activity. Stalls are being set up, decorations hung, and the clatter of pots and pans resonates from the direction of the open glade near "Beastly Bites," where the town feast will be held. I make my way there, dodging a group of excitable fairy children, who zoom past on miniature broomsticks.

As I approach "Beastly Bites," I see the chef, Caelan—who I know now is a fire demon— directing a team of helpers. His flame-red hair dances like a living fire atop his head, and his eyes glow with enthusiasm.

"Ah, Candice," he calls out when he spots me. "Perfect timing. We need another pair of hands to sort through these deliveries."

I nod, rolling up my sleeves. "Happy to help. Where do you want me?"

He points to a pile of crates near the back of a large table. Everything is being sorted and prepared open-air today, but there are no insects hovering. I assume someone cast a repellant charm. "Those just came in from Puckley's farm. Start unpacking and sorting, please. Vegetables on the left and fruits on the right."

I set to work, marveling at the vibrant colors and unusual shapes of the produce. Puckley's farm was simply too large for me to have seen all these on my tour. Some of the vegetables pulse with a faint inner light, while others change color as I touch them.

"These are amazing," I say to no one in particular.

A deep, rumbling voice responds from behind me. "Wait until you taste them."

I turn to find Ronan standing there. My heart does a little flip at the sight of him, which I quickly try to suppress. "Ronan," I say, hoping my voice sounds steady. "Are you here to help too?"

He nods, moving to stand beside me. "Caelan asked me to lend a hand with the heavy lifting since you and I finished the decorating yesterday."

We work side by side, unpacking crates and sorting produce, as Caelan calls out various menu ideas. That's when the clash begins.

"For the main course, I'm thinking a grand roast beast," says the chef. "With a side of bloodroot mash and cannibal carrots."

I freeze, my hand halfway to a shimmering eggplant. "Cannibal carrots?"

Caelan waves a hand dismissively. "They only eat other vegetables. They're perfectly safe for human consumption."

I shake my head. "That's not... I mean, I'm actually a vegetarian."

The kitchen goes quiet for a moment. Ronan looks at me, his eyes wide with surprise.

"A vegetarian?" Caelan repeats, sounding perplexed. "But... how do you survive without meat?"

I straighten up, feeling a need to defend my lifestyle. "There are plenty of delicious and nutritious plant-based options. In fact, I'd be happy to suggest some vegetarian dishes for the feast."

Ronan clears his throat. "Caelan, perhaps we could offer both options? A meat dish and a vegetarian alternative?"

Caelan considers this for a moment, then nods. "Yes, yes, that could work. Candice, what would you suggest for a vegetarian main course?"

I think for a moment. "How about a hearty mushroom stew? We could use some of these amazing magical vegetables. Maybe those color-changing squash and the glowing mushrooms?"

Caelan's eyes light up—literally, as small flames dance in his pupils. "Ooh, yes. And we could enchant the stew to change flavors with each bite. Brilliant."

While we continue discussing the menu, I notice Ronan watching me with curiosity. "I've never met a vegetarian before other than some of the sprites and pixies. Is it a common practice in the human world?"

I nod. "It's becoming more popular, yes. Some people do it for health reasons, and others for ethical or environmental concerns." I frown. "I do it because I got a tick bite when I was little that made me allergic to certain proteins. Most meat literally makes me sick."

Ronan looks thoughtful. "Interesting...and sorry about that. In lycan culture, meat is a crucial part of our diet. We need the protein to maintain our strength, especially during transformations."

As if to emphasize his point, he reaches into a nearby cooler and pulls out a raw steak. Without hesitation, he takes a big bite, sharp teeth tearing through the meat.

I stare with fascination and horror coursing through me. The sight of blood dripping down his chin makes my stomach churn, but I also recall the taste of a hamburger sharper than I have in years and wish I could have one. Alas, it's not worth the illness that follows when a portobello burger is a reasonable substitute.

Ronan notices my expression and quickly wipes his mouth. "Sorry," he says, looking sheepish. "I forget that can be off-putting to humans."

"It's okay," I say, trying to sound nonchalant. "You're probably an obligate carnivore, right? Like a cat or a dog?"

The moment the words leave my mouth, I realize how they might sound. Ronan raises an eyebrow, and I giggle at the absurdity of the situation.

"I mean, not that you're like a pet or anything," I quickly add, my cheeks burning as I imagine him curled up on my lap watching a movie. There's nothing fuzzy or platonic about that image. "I just meant... oh, never mind."

To my relief, he chuckles. "I understand, and you're not entirely wrong. Lycans do have certain dietary needs that are closer to wolves than humans. Dogs aren't obligate carnivores either, by the way, but they do need most of their diet to come from protein. Same for lycans."

Our gazes meet, and for a moment, I forget about the raw meat and the dietary differences. Instead, I'm wondering what other differences there are between lycans and humans. My gaze wants to dip...southward...but I fight the urge and make myself maintain eye contact. There's warmth in Ronan's gaze that makes my heart skip a beat and almost makes me forget my curiosity about his anatomy.

Almost...

Caelan's voice breaks the moment. "All right, you two. Less chatting, more sorting. We've got a feast to prepare."

We both jump slightly, turning our attention back to the task at hand. As we continue working, I keep stealing glances at Ronan. Despite our differences, there's something about him that intrigues me.

The outdoor kitchen buzzes with activity while we prepare for the feast. Caelan orchestrates the chaos like a maestro, his fiery hair flickering with excitement. I focus on preparing the vegetarian dishes, determined to show plant-based food can be delicious.

As I chop some color-changing squash, Ronan watches me. He's preparing a marinade for the roast beast, his powerful hands mixing herbs with practiced ease. He tells me more about the people around us and the town while we work. until a loud pop on the other side of the kitchen interrupts our conversation.

We turn to see Caelan frantically waving his hands over a pot that's emitting rainbow-colored smoke. "Oops," he says, grinning sheepishly. "Looks like the flavor-changing enchantment was a bit too strong. This might go from blueberry to beets. That's too much, but don't worry. I'll fix it."

I laugh at the sight of the normally composed fire demon chef looking so flustered. Ronan joins in, his deep chuckle harmonizing with my giggles. As the day progresses, I enjoy the preparations. The magical ingredients are fascinating to work with, and there's a sense of community in the kitchen that warms my heart. Even Caelan's occasional magical mishaps add to the charm of the experience.

By late afternoon, the feast is starting to come together. The air is filled with mouth-watering aromas, both familiar and exotic. I've just finished putting the final touches on a shimmering salad when Ronan approaches me again.

"Candice," he says, looking a bit nervous. "I was wondering if you'd like to take a break and go for a walk? There's something I'd like to show you."

I glance at Caelan, who waves us off with a flaming hand. "Go, go. You've both earned a break. I won't need you again until dinner, when we feast."

We step away from the bustling outdoor kitchen, and I realize how much I've been enjoying my time in Evershift Haven. Despite the initial shock, and the occasional clashes of culture, there's something magical about this place that goes beyond the obvious enchantments.

"Where are we going?" I ask, curiosity getting the better of me.

He smiles, a hint of mystery in his blue eyes. "You'll see. It's a special place that I think you'll appreciate, especially given your connection to nature." Ronan leads me toward the edge of town, where the Whispering Woods begin. The trees seem to sway toward us as we approach, rustling their leaves with what sounds suspiciously like whispered greetings.

When we walk deeper into the woods, the air grows thick with an otherworldly energy. I strain my ears, catching whispers that sound eerily like voices. "Ronan," I say, my voice hushed. "Are the trees...talking?"

He nods with a smile. "They are. Listen closely."

I concentrate, and suddenly, the whispers become clearer. To my amazement, I hear snippets of conversation and...poetry?

"Fair maiden with hair of gold,
In our woods, a story unfolds.
With the lycan strong and true,
A tale of love, both old and new."

My cheeks flush when I realize the trees are talking about us.

Ronan chuckles. "They seem to like you," he says. "The Whispering Woods don't talk to just anyone, you know. Only those with an affinity for greenery can hear them directly."

I raise an eyebrow. "Really? So not everyone can hear this?"

Ronan shakes his head. "No. Throk can hear them, and I can, of course, but even Suzette can't. You must have a special connection to nature."

The revelation makes me pause. I've always loved plants, but I never imagined it could be anything more than a hobby. Could there be more to my connection with nature than I realized?

As we continue walking, the trees' whispers grow more insistent. Their branches seem to reach out, gently brushing against us as if trying to push us closer together.

"Young love, so sweet and shy,
Beneath our boughs, don't be sly.
A kiss, a touch, don't hesitate,
For in this moment, seal your fate."

My eyes widen as I process the words. Are the trees telling us to kiss? I glance at Ronan, who looks equally surprised and...is that a hint of hope in his eyes?

For a moment, I consider it. He is undeniably attractive, and there's something about him that draws me in, but the suddenness of it all, coupled with the strangeness of our surroundings, makes me hesitate.

"I, uh... I think I need a break," I stammer, taking a step back. "And maybe a drink. How about we head to 'The Enchanted Espresso?'"

His expression flickers with disappointment before he nods. "Of course. Let's head back."

As I turn to walk away, I hear Ronan's deep voice behind me, chiding the trees. "Now look what you've done. You've scared her off."

The trees rustle in response, their tone almost apologetic. He chuckles before following me as I pretend I didn't hear their exchange.

We make our way back toward town, the silence between us charged with unspoken words. The Whispering Woods gradually give way to the more manicured landscape of Evershift Haven, and I'm both relieved and oddly disappointed to be leaving the magical forest behind.

Approaching "The Enchanted Espresso," I sneak a glance at Ronan. His profile is strong and defined, and his fur gleams in the late afternoon sunlight. I wonder what it would feel like to run my fingers through it.

Chapter 5

THE BELL ABOVE THE door of "The Enchanted Espresso" chimes as Ronan and I step inside. The cozy interior wraps around us like a warm blanket with the scent of freshly ground coffee beans and cinnamon filling the air. Plush armchairs in rich autumnal hues invite patrons to sink into them, while floating candles cast a soft, flickering glow over the room.

Behind the counter, Bella Brewster's curly leaf-red hair frizzes with magical energy. Her eyes, currently a warm amber, twinkle as she spots us. "If it isn't my favorite new human and our resident lumberjack? What can I get for you two today?"

I glance at the menu board, which seems to be writing and erasing itself. "I'm not sure. What do you recommend?"

Her grin widens, revealing dimples in her rosy cheeks. "Oh, I've got just the thing for you both. How about our special fall drink? The Autumn Glow Latte."

Ronan nods with interest. "Sounds perfect. Two of those, please."

As Bella busies herself with the espresso machine, which hums and purrs like a contented cat, I turn to Ronan. "So, what makes this latte so special?"

"I don't know yet." He leans in, lowering his voice conspiratorially. "Bella's drinks always have a little extra magic to them. I'm curious to see what this one does."

Before I can ask for clarification, she returns with two steaming mugs. The foam on top swirls and shifts, forming an intricate design. I bend closer, eyes widening as I recognize the scene depicted in the latte art. It's Ronan and me, walking through the woods we'd explored earlier. The foam figures move, brushing their hands against each other. As I watch, they turn toward each other, leaning in for what looks like a kiss.

Heat rises to my cheeks, and I quickly grab a spoon, stirring the foam away before Ronan can see. "That's, uh, some impressive latte art," I say with a stammer.

Bella winks at me. "Oh, you haven't seen anything yet. Take a sip."

I lift the mug to my lips. The first taste is a concerto of flavors—rich espresso, creamy milk, and a blend of spices that dance on my tongue. As I swallow, a peculiar warmth spreads through my body. "Oh." I exclaim, looking down at my hands. My skin seems to be glowing from within, taking on a warm, golden hue. Flecks of gold shimmer across my skin, reminiscent of sunlight filtering through autumn leaves.

Ronan chuckles, his own skin now radiating the same warm glow. "Bella, you've outdone yourself this time."

Bella preens, her hair frizzing even more with pride. "The Autumn Glow Latte. It gives you that perfect fall golden hour look for about an hour. Quite popular for selfies, I must say."

I catch my reflection in a nearby mirror. The effect is stunning—I look as if I'm bathed in perpetual sunset light, my skin glowing and my hair shimmering with golden highlights.

"This is incredible," I say, turning back to Ronan. The sight of him nearly takes my breath away. The golden light emphasizes the strong lines of his face, and his blue eyes seem even more vibrant against his shimmering fur.

"You look beautiful," he says softly.

I duck my head, suddenly shy. "So do you. I mean, handsome. You look handsome."

Bella clears her throat, a knowing smile on her face. "Why don't you two take a seat by the window? The sunlight will really make that glow pop."

We make our way to the cozy nook by a window, settling into plush armchairs that seem to mold perfectly to our bodies. Outside, the streets of Evershift Haven bustle with activity, the golden glow of our skin drawing curious and appreciative glances from passersby.

"So," I say, taking another sip of my latte, "Is this a typical day in Evershift Haven? Magical lattes and glowing skin?"

He laughs. "Every day here is different. That's part of the charm. You never know what kind of magic you'll encounter."

I nod, my mind spinning with the possibilities. "It's all so overwhelming. Beautiful, but overwhelming. How do you ever get used to it?"

"You don't really, but that's the beauty of it. There's always something new to discover, or some new wonder to experience. It keeps life exciting."

As if to prove his point, a group of fairies flits past our window, leaving trails of sparkling dust in their wake. The dust settles on the cobblestones, forming intricate, swirling patterns.

"I can see why you love it here," I say, turning back to him. The warmth in his eyes matches the glow of his skin, and I sway forward slightly.

"I'm glad you're here to see it," he says softly. He moves his hand across the table, brushing his fingers against mine. The touch sends a jolt through me, more potent than any magical latte.

We sit in comfortable silence for a moment, sipping our drinks and basking in the warm glow. The attraction between us seems heightened by the magical effect of the latte. Every glance and every accidental touch feels charged with possibility.

He sets down his mug, clearly finished. "What would you like to see next? Evershift Haven has no shortage of wonders to offer, and we can spare a little more time before the feast begins."

I consider for a moment. "Surprise me. Show me your favorite place in town."

His grin is wide and eager. "I know just the spot. Finish your latte. We've got a bit of a walk ahead of us."

As I drain the last drops of my Autumn Glow Latte, I get a thrill of excitement. Whatever magical adventure awaits us next, I'm ready for it.

A short time later, I follow Ronan through the winding paths of Evershift Haven, the golden glow from our Autumn Latte still shimmering on our skin. Enchanted leaves crunch beneath our feet, releasing bursts of cinnamon and nutmeg scents into the crisp air. As we leave the town center, a gentle mist rises around our ankles with cool tendrils curling up our legs.

"Where exactly are we headed?" I ask, my curiosity piqued by the secretive glint in his eye.

He grins, a flash of white teeth against his dark fur. "You'll see. Just listen."

I strain my ears, and soon, a gentle lapping sound reaches me, like tiny waves kissing a shore. The path narrows, and his broad shoulders barely fit between the trees. He turns to make sure I'm still behind him, his eyes gleaming with a hint of animal shine in the fading light.

"Here we are," he says, his voice a low rumble of excitement. He reaches out, gently pushing aside a curtain of silvery willow branches with his clawed hand. "The Luminous Lagoon."

As the branches part, I gasp. The lagoon stretches out before us, its surface so still it looks like polished glass. The twilight sky reflects perfectly in its depths, but it's not the mirrored image that steals my breath.

Colors dance across the water—vibrant swirls of sapphire, emerald, and amethyst. They pulse and shift, intertwining and separating in a mesmerizing ballet. It's as if the northern lights have fallen from the sky and decided to make this lagoon their new home.

I'm unable to look away from the spectacle. "It's beautiful."

He nods. "The colors change with the phases of the moon, among other reasons. Tonight's show is courtesy of the waxing crescent."

I take a step closer to the water's edge, feeling the damp earth give slightly beneath my feet. The mist swirls around us, carrying the scent of water lilies and magic. As I watch, a tendril of green light seems to reach out toward me then playfully retreats back into the dance.

"Can we touch it?" I ask, my hand already half-extended.

He chuckles. "Go ahead. The water spirits are always eager to meet new friends."

"It's beautiful," I whisper again, afraid to speak too loudly and break the spell.

His sharp teeth glint in the magical light. "Wait until you see this." He leads me to the water's edge and kneels. "Watch." He dips his hand into the lagoon. The water around his fingers immediately turns a deep, rich blue. Ripples of the color spread outward, mixing with the other hues on the surface.

"What does that mean?" I ask, fascinated.

"Blue represents calm and contentment. The lagoon reflects our emotions. It's different for everyone who touches it."

I hesitate before lowering my hand into the cool water. The effect is instantaneous. A vibrant purple blooms around my fingers, spreading out in mesmerizing patterns. "Oh." I exclaim, surprised by the intensity of the color. "What does purple mean?"

He looks at me with speculation. "Purple typically represents amorous feelings."

Heat rushes to my cheeks, and I snatch back my hand. "That can't be right. The water must be malfunctioning or something."

He chuckles. "The lagoon doesn't lie, Candice. It simply reflects what's in our hearts."

I cross my arms, trying to ignore the butterflies in my stomach. "Well, it's wrong this time. I'm not feeling...amorous."

"No?" he asks, clearly teasing. He leans closer, and I catch a whiff of his scent—pine and earth and something wild. "Are you sure about that?" Before I can respond, he dips his hand back into the water. To my shock, the liquid around his fingers turns the same vibrant purple as mine.

"Oh..." My eyes widen as I look from the water to his face.

His expression is vulnerable. "I guess the lagoon reveals my feelings too."

We stare at each other, the air between us charged with possibility. The golden glow from Bella's latte seems to intensify just before it starts to fade, casting Ronan in an ethereal light. His fur shimmers, and his eyes are impossibly bright.

I lean toward him, drawn by an irresistible pull. He meets me halfway, gently cupping my cheek in his large hand. Our faces are inches apart when I hesitate, suddenly unsure. "I... I've never kissed anyone with a muzzle before."

His eyes crinkle with amusement. "There's a first time for everything in Evershift Haven." He traces my jawline with extraordinary gentleness, those dangerous claws somehow feeling like silk against my skin as he tilts his head, compensating for his lupine features with practiced grace. "Trust me," he whispers, caressing my face with his warm breath.

Our lips connect—a study in contrasts. His are covered in that same velvet-soft fur that masks his powerful form, radiating heat that makes my knees weak. My own lips part slightly, surrendering to the gentle pressure.

The kiss starts feather-light, almost questioning, while we learn each other's shapes and boundaries. Electric shivers race from my scalp to my toes, making my fingers tremble as they find their way into the thicker fur at the back of his neck. It's impossibly plush between my fingers, like burying my hands in the warmest, softest wool.

I press closer, taking in his woodsy scent as the kiss deepens. With my fingertips, I discover the solid strength of his neck beneath all that softness, and I hold on like he's my anchor to reality. When we finally pull apart, we're both a little breathless. The glow from the latte seems to have further intensified, making our skin shimmer like we've been dusted with gold. With a slight flicker, it abruptly disappears, leaving us in much darker surroundings with the sun starting to set, and the trees shading us.

"Whoa," I say, tracing my tingling lips with a finger.

Ronan grins, looking equally affected. "Yep."

We stand there without speaking for a minute with neither of us stepping back, caught in the moment and the magic surrounding us. The lagoon continues its colorful dance, now dominated by swirls of deep, rich purple.

"We should get back to help Caelan with the rest of preparations for tomorrow," he says with regret.

I nod but then blink as the wind suddenly picks up. Leaves blow around us, and a small waterspout forms. The sky gets abruptly dark. "What's happening?"

He frowns. "Either an unexpected storm, or Grizelda's magic has gone haywire again."

Chapter 6

THE SKY DARKENS RAPIDLY as thick clouds roll in like an angry tide. A crack of thunder shakes the air, and fat raindrops begin to pelt us. Ronan grabs my hand, his fur already darkening with moisture.

"My cabin's just over there," he shouts over the growing wind. "We can wait out the storm."

We sprint across the increasingly muddy ground as rain lashes our faces. Lightning flashes, illuminating the path ahead in stark white. By the time we reach Ronan's cabin, about a quarter-mile from the Luminous Lagoon, we're both soaked to the bone.

He turns the doorknob, his claws clicking against the metal, and the door swings open. Clearly, locking doors isn't a big concern here. I'm relieved when we tumble inside, dripping onto the wooden floor. The interior is dim, lit only by the gray light filtering through rain-streaked windows.

"Quite a storm," I say, wringing water from my hair. "Is it always like this?"

Ronan shakes himself, sending droplets flying. "Not usually. This feels different. More intense than a natural storm, so I'm guessing Grizelda's pregnancy sickness is making her magic glitch again." He moves to the fireplace, arranging logs with practiced ease. "You should get out of those wet clothes. The bathroom's through there, so feel free to have a warm shower. I'll find you something dry to wear."

I nod gratefully and squelch my way to the bathroom. It's small but cozy, with a claw-foot tub and standing shower attachment and a mirror that seems to ripple like water when I look at it too long. I peel off my sodden clothes, hanging them over the towel rod before stepping into a hot shower. I keep it brief, knowing he's waiting to warm up too.

I'm just turning off the water when there's a soft knock at the door. "I've got some clothes for you," he says. "I'll leave them outside."

"Thanks," I say, wrapping myself in a fluffy towel. When I peek out, I find a neatly folded flannel shirt and a pair of sweatpants. The shirt smells like pine and something uniquely Ronan. I slip it on, the soft fabric enveloping me like a warm hug. I skip the sweatpants, which are laughably too big, even with a drawstring waist.

When I emerge from the bathroom, the cabin is transformed. A fire crackles merrily in the hearth, casting dancing shadows on the walls. Ronan has changed into dry clothes as well, but his fur is still slightly damp and tousled. I guess he decided not to wait for the shower.

"Feel better?" he asks, glancing up from where he's arranging blankets on the couch.

I nod, padding over to join him. "Much. Thanks for the shirt." I look down at the navy and kelly-green plaid shirt, running my fingers across the hem as it strikes me that he's recently worn this. Wearing his shirt is almost like having his arms around me.

"It suits you," he says with a small smile. "Hungry? I've got some vegetable barley soup warming on the stove."

My stomach growls in response, and we both laugh. "I'll take that as a yes," he says, moving to the kitchen area.

I take the opportunity to look around the cabin. It's a single room, with the kitchen area to one side and a large bed tucked into an alcove on the other. Bookshelves line the walls, filled with an eclectic mix of titles. A few framed photos catch my eye—Ronan with what must be his family since they're all lycans.

"This is a nice place," I say as he returns with two steaming bowls. "Very...you."

He hands me a bowl and settles beside me on the couch. "Thanks. It's not much, but it's home."

We eat in companionable silence for a while, accompanied only by the sounds of the crackling fire and the storm raging outside. The soup is hearty and delicious, warming me from the inside out. "So," I say, setting aside my empty bowl. "How long do these magical storms usually last?"

He frowns slightly. "It's hard to say." A particularly loud crack of thunder makes me jump. "Don't worry. We're safe here."

I look down at our joined hands, my much smaller one nearly disappearing in his large, furred grip. "Can I ask you something?"

"Of course."

"Earlier, at the lagoon…when the water changed color. What did that mean to you?"

He looks at me intently. "It meant…hope. Possibility. Something I haven't felt in a long time."

My heart starts galloping. "What do you feel now?"

He cups my cheek, his touch impossibly gentle for someone so strong. "I—"

Another crash of thunder, loud enough to rattle the windows, interrupts him. We both jump, and the moment is broken. He clears his throat, dropping his hand. "I should check the windows and make sure everything's secure."

I nod, trying to hide my disappointment. As he moves around the cabin, I curl up on the couch. The storm rages outside, wind howling and rain lashing against the windows. I wrap the blanket tighter around my shoulders, watching Ronan. His movements are graceful despite his large frame, with each action purposeful and efficient.

"I think we're all set," he says, returning to the couch. "The storm doesn't seem to be letting up anytime soon."

I nod, shifting to make room for him. "It's extreme. I've never seen anything like it."

He settles beside me, radiating warmth even through my blanket. "Magical storms can be unpredictable. They tap into the energy of the land itself."

"That sounds…powerful," I say, struggling to wrap my mind around the concept. "Is it dangerous?"

He shakes his head. "Not usually. Just intense. The cabin's warded against magical interference. We're safe here."

A comfortable silence falls between us, broken only by the crackling fire, and the storm's fury outside. I study his profile, liking the way the firelight plays across his features. "Can I ask you something?" I say, breaking the silence.

Ronan turns to me. "Of course."

"Do you ever think about leaving Evershift Haven?"

He sighs, a low rumble in his chest. "Yes, but it's too complicated. You've probably noticed I'm not like the werewolves in your stories."

I nod, remembering the tales of men transforming into wolves under the full moon. "You're always like this, right?"

"Yes. Lycans are...stuck, I suppose you could say. We can't fully shift between wolf and human forms. This is our natural state." He holds up a hand, flexing his clawed fingers. "It makes blending into the human world challenging."

"I see," I say softly. "So Evershift Haven is..."

"A place where I can be myself without fear or judgment. My pack has been here for generations. We're part of the fabric of this community."

I reach out, hesitating for a moment before placing my hand on his furred arm. "That must be both comforting and limiting."

He nods while, looking at where my hand rests. "It is. I'm grateful for the safety and acceptance Evershift provides, but sometimes, I wonder about the world beyond. The human world."

He smiles, a flash of sharp teeth that I now find endearing rather than intimidating. "Occasionally, the best parts of the human world come to me. I'm curious by nature, and you intrigue me, Candice."

I flush at his words. "I'm not that interesting."

"I disagree," he says. "Tell me something about your life in Chicago. Something you love."

I think for a moment as memories of the bustling city flash through my mind. "There's this little farmers' market I go to every weekend. It's nothing fancy, just a handful of local farmers selling their produce, but there's something magical about it. The way the vegetables are arranged in neat rows, still covered in bits of soil, the smell of fresh herbs and ripe fruit..." I trail off with a happy sigh. "The farmers know me by name now. They always save the best tomatoes for me."

As I speak, he moves closer. "That sounds wonderful. Do you grow things yourself? I think you mentioned an herb garden?"

I laugh softly. "Not really. Just a few herbs on my windowsill, and some containers on my patio. My apartment doesn't exactly have space for a garden, but..." I trail off, suddenly self-conscious.

"But what?" he prompts gently.

I inhale and exhale a couple of times, bracing myself to admit something I haven't even told my sister. "Promise not to laugh?"

He places a hand over his heart, the gesture solemn despite the twinkle in his eyes. "Lycan's honor."

"Okay. The truth is, I've always dreamed of being a farmer. Not just growing a few tomatoes, but really farming. Working the land, watching things grow from seed to harvest, and being self-reliant. There's something so pure about it. So connected to nature."

I expect Ronan to chuckle at my city-girl farming fantasies, but his expression is thoughtful. "That's a beautiful dream. Have you ever considered pursuing it?"

I shake my head. "It's not practical. I have a career in event planning. It's what I'm good at. Farming is just a silly daydream."

"Dreams aren't silly," he says firmly. "Especially not here in Evershift Haven. This is a place where dreams can become reality, if you're brave enough to chase them."

His words stir something in me, a longing I've tried to bury beneath practicality and expectations. "Maybe," I say softly, "But it's not like I can just quit my job and buy a farm."

"Why not?" he asks. "Evershift Haven has some of the most fertile land in any realm, and we're always looking for new farmers to help feed the magical community."

I stare at him, considering the possibilities. "Are you serious?"

He nods with excitement. "Absolutely. In fact, there's a plot of land not far from here that's been lying fallow for years. It's said to be blessed by earth sprites. With a little work, it could be transformed into a thriving farm. My family also has some land," he says, almost shyly.

Excitement flares at the idea. "That would be wonderful, but I don't know the first thing about magical farming, and I can't just abandon my life in Chicago."

"You could learn," he says. "And as for Chicago... That's a decision only you can make but know you'd be welcome here. More than welcome."

The intensity in his gaze makes my breath catch, and I'm sure he's referring to his cabin even more than the town. Outside, a particularly loud crack of thunder booms, making the windows rattle. I jump, instinctively moving closer to him.

Without hesitation, he wraps his arms around me, pulling me against his broad chest. The steady beat of his heart is a counterpoint to the storm's fury. "I've got you," he whispers, and his breath is warm against my scalp.

I look up, meeting his gaze. The air between us seems to crackle with more than just the storm's energy. "Ronan," I whisper, bringing my hand up to rest on his cheek.

He leans into my touch, briefly closing his eyelids. When they open again, they're dark with desire. "Candice," he says softly, and then his lips are on mine.

The kiss is gentle at first, almost hesitant, but as I respond, wrapping my arms around his neck, it deepens. One of his hands presses against my back, pulling me closer until I'm practically in his lap. I run my fingers through his fur, marveling at its softness.

We break apart, panting slightly. He rests his forehead against mine. "Candice," he says again, his voice husky with need. "If you want me to stop, tell me now. Once we start, I might not be able to hold back. You test my control in ways no one ever has."

I swallow hard. My body is already responding to his nearness, nipples tightening while heat pools between my thighs. "Don't stop," I say firmly.

That's all the encouragement he needs. He kisses me again, harder this time, titling his muzzle so that our lips touch before he deepens the kiss once more. His tongue surges into my mouth, and it has more texture than a human's, but it's exotic and pleasurable. I moan softly, pressing against him.

He growls in response, the sound vibrating through my entire body. One large hand cups my breast, kneading it gently. I gasp as he rolls my nipple between his thumb and forefinger, sending sparks of pleasure shooting through me.

His other hand slides down my back, cupping my ass and squeezing it firmly. I whimper, grinding against him. His cock is straining against his pants, and I long to free it and see what to expect from a lycan lover. Can we even physically...fit together? My sister is in love with an orc, so inter-species mating should be possible, but I'm suddenly anxious and curious.

I ease back, breaking our kiss while unbuttoning his plaid shirt. His fur springs free, and I run my fingers through his lush pelt. "You feel so different. It's good," I add hastily when he frowns. "It's just new to me."

"I understand." He nuzzles my neck. "I promise you'll enjoy every minute of being with me."

I believe him. My body is already aching for him, and he must be able to smell my arousal. I push his shirt off his shoulders, baring his chest. He shrugs out of it, letting it fall to the floor. Gliding my hand down his chest and to his abs, I feel the hard muscle underneath the soft fur. He's built like a Greek god, and I can't wait to explore every inch of him.

I reach for the waistband of his jeans and fumble with the button. He helps me, undoing it quickly and pushing them down. His cock springs free, and I stare at it in awe. It's huge, easily ten inches long, and thicker than anything I've seen before, but it's not the size that surprises me. No, it's the knot at the base of his shaft. It's bigger than a tennis ball, and I wonder how it will fit inside me.

He must notice my apprehension because he says, "We don't have to do anything you're not comfortable with, and I can stop before...the knot. You probably can't take all of it our first time anyway."

I smile up at him and lick my lips. "That sounds like a challenge...but I like the sound of first time."

He laughs. "First of many, I hope." He pulls me closer again, his fingers working the buttons on the plaid shirt he loaned me. I'm completely bare underneath. Even my panties and bra were soaked by the deluge.

I shiver with anticipation as he pushes the shirt off my shoulders, exposing my breasts. They're small, barely a handful, but he cups them reverently, stroking my nipples with his thumbs. The sensation sends sparks of pleasure straight to my pussy, which is already dripping wet.

His nostrils flare, and he growls softly. "You smell amazing."

I blush at his confirmation that he can smell my arousal. "So do you," I say shyly, inhaling deeply. His scent is musky and masculine, and it makes me want to rub myself all over him.

He kisses me again, harder this time, his tongue invading my mouth possessively. I moan into the kiss, pressing my body against his. His cock is rock-hard now, and I feel the heat radiating from it. I grind against him, desperate for friction while grasping it with my palm.

I swallow, a bit intimidated. There's so much of it. "It's big," I whisper.

"Too big?" he asks, sounding worried.

"No, just...bigger than what I'm used to." I wink. "Furrier too." The fur is mostly around his balls and knot, but it's thick and plush like the rest covering his body.

He chuckles. "The fur doesn't bother you?"

"Not at all. I think it's sexy." I slowly stroke his cock, feeling the velvety skin slide over the hardness beneath. He groans, thrusting into my hand.

"Candice..." His voice is strained. "If you keep doing that, I won't be able to control myself."

"Good," I murmur, continuing to stroke him. "I want you to lose control."

He growls, grabbing my wrist and pulling my hand away from his cock. "Then get on your knees."

My heart pounds as I sink to my knees in front of him. I've never tried to take such a large cock in my mouth, but I want to please him. I look up at him, waiting for further instruction. I expect him to ask for a blowjob.

Instead, he walks around behind me, getting to his knees as well. For a second, the tip of his cock glides down my slit, but then he's moving farther away while urging me to bend forward across the couch. When he cups my hips and lifts me, his intent is clear.

A second later, his rough, raspy tongue slides between my folds. I gasp, gripping the cushions tightly as he begins to lick me. His tongue is long and thick, and he uses it expertly, swirling it around my clit before dipping inside me. I moan, rocking back against him, wanting more.

He pulls away briefly, chuckling. "Eager, aren't you? Don't worry, I'll give you everything you need." Then his tongue is back, licking and sucking at my pussy until I'm trembling with pleasure.

He grips my ass cheeks firmly, spreading them apart so he can reach every inch of me. I cry out as he pushes his tongue deeper inside me, fucking me with it. My orgasm builds quickly, and soon I'm screaming as waves of ecstasy crash over me.

As I come, he continues to lap at my juices, drinking them greedily. Finally, he withdraws, panting heavily. "You taste amazing," he says huskily. "I could eat you forever."

I turn my head to look at him over my shoulder. "That was incredible, but now I really want to feel you inside me."

He grins wickedly. "Oh, don't worry, little human. You will."

With that promise, he moves closer, positioning himself behind me. His cock presses against my entrance, and I hold up a hand. "Do we need to use protection or something? I'm on the pill and all, but magic...? Can a lycan even get a human pregnant?"

"Not most places, but anything is possible in Evershift Haven." His tip enters me slowly, making us both moan. "Your pill should protect you."

I nod, relaxing as he sinks deeper inside me. He feels huge, stretching me wide open. I whimper softly, trying to adjust to his size.

He pauses, letting me catch my breath. "Are you okay?"

"Yes," I whisper. "Just...go slowly."

He nods, continuing to push forward steadily but gently. Soon, he's filling me completely, and I cry out in pleasure. His fur cradles my ass, and his knot presses against my entrance. I can't yet take it, but he doesn't seem bothered as he withdraws and lightly thrusts into me again.

My cries grow louder as he picks up speed, pounding into me harder and faster. I cling to the couch cushions, bracing myself against his powerful thrusts. I tremble as another orgasm builds deeply within me. He growls, tightly gripping my hips as he slams into me.

Then suddenly, he stops moving. I glance over my shoulder to see what's wrong, but he just smiles at me. "Ready?"

Before I can respond, he pushes his knot into me, forcing it past my tight ring of muscle. I expect pain, but it's only a slight twinge before intense pleasure floods through me. I arch my back, pushing against him as he begins to move again. This time, he sets a slower pace, gently rocking his hips as he fills me completely.

The pressure inside me grows until I think I might explode. Then, without warning, I do. My vision goes white as ecstasy consumes me. I shout his name, clenching around him as my climax crashes through me. He roars, burying his face in my neck as he comes too, flooding me with his hot seed. I collapse onto the couch, panting heavily as aftershocks ripple through me.

After a few minutes, I come to my senses and realize he's still hard inside me. "Is that normal?"

He grunts, sounding more animal than man for a moment. "Yes. It will take several orgasms before the knot softens, allowing me to pull out."

I look over my shoulder, giving him a look of exasperation but also amusement. "You might have mentioned that earlier. I don't want to stay on my knees for hours."

His lips curl into a smile, showing off his fangs. "We can change positions if you'd like."

I consider this for a moment, then nod. "Okay."

He lifts me easily, shifting us so that he's sitting on the couch with me straddling his lap, facing away from him. His knot remains buried inside me, stretching me open wide. I settle back against his chest, sighing contentedly as he wraps his arms around me. We sit like that for a while, enjoying the closeness and intimacy of our position. Eventually, his cock begins to swell again, growing thicker and harder inside me.

"Are you ready for another round?" He cups my breasts as he asks while burying his muzzle against my neck.

I yelp with shock, not pain, when he nips me there, and nod enthusiastically. "Yes."

He chuckles. "Good girl."

With that, he begins thrusting again, setting a slow and steady pace. I moan softly, letting myself relax into his embrace as he takes control. As the storm rages outside, we lose ourselves in each other, exploring this new, exciting connection. With each kiss, each tender touch, and each thrust of our bodies, I'm falling deeper into the magic of Evershift Haven—and into Ronan's arms.

Chapter 7

I WAKE UP EARLY, NOTING Ronan is gone, but he left a note on his pillow:

Candice,

Sorry. Caelan called. The weather has cleared enough that we can have the feast today. It obviously got cancelled last night. He needs new, dry wood for the wood-fired ovens, and you looked too peaceful to wake.

Ronan

I find my clothes from yesterday, neatly folded on his dryer, and dress as excitement builds for the upcoming Thanksgiving feast—and for seeing my lycan lover again.

The air crackles with anticipation while I make my way to the beautiful glen where the town has gathered. Autumn leaves dance on a gentle breeze, their vibrant hues a perfect backdrop for the festive decorations.

Pumpkins of every size and shape line the pathways, and some are carved with intricate designs that seem to shift when I'm not looking directly at them. Cornucopias overflow with an abundance of magical produce—shimmering apples, iridescent corn, and berries that sparkle like jewels.

I spot Grizelda near the center of the glen, her wild mane of silver-streaked purple hair moving as if it has a life of its own. She's wearing flowing robes adorned with mysterious symbols that seem to glow faintly. As I approach, I notice her hand resting on her slightly rounded belly.

"Grizelda." I say, waving. "Everything looks amazing."

She turns, her vibrant purple eyes lighting up. "Candice, darling. So glad you could make it. Are you ready for a truly magical Thanksgiving?"

I laugh, still not entirely used to how casually everyone here uses the word 'magical.' "As ready as I'll ever be. Is there anything with which I can help?"

She shakes her head, a mischievous glint in her eye. "Oh, no, dear. I'm feeling much better today and have something special planned. Just you wait and see." She raises her arms, preparing to cast a spell, when suddenly, she turns pale. Her hands drop to her stomach and she sways slightly.

"Grizelda?" I ask, concerned. "Are you okay?"

She waves me off with one hand, the other still pressed to her belly. "I'm fine. Just a bit of morning sickness. Nothing to worry about. Now, where was I? Ah, yes, the enhancement spell for our feast."

Before I can protest, she begins chanting in a language I don't understand. The air around us shimmers and pulsates with energy, but something seems off. Her voice wavers, and the magical energy surrounding her flickers erratically.

Suddenly, chaos erupts.

A nearby apple pie levitates off its table, spinning like a frisbee before zooming away. I duck just in time to avoid being hit by it.

"Oh, my," says Grizelda with surprise.

All around us, food comes to life. A giant bowl of mashed potatoes begins to bubble and expand, spilling over the edges of its container and oozing across the table like lava. Guests leap back, their shouts of surprise mingling with nervous laughter.

I watch in disbelief as a group of pumpkin pies rise into the air, hovering like a fleet of orange UFOs. They zip around, narrowly missing the heads of startled townsfolk.

"Grizelda," I say, trying to keep my voice calm, "What's happening?"

She looks both amused and embarrassed. "It seems my spell didn't quite go as planned. Pregnancy does tend to affect a witch's magic sometimes." She lowers her voice, looking pained when she adds, "Especially at my age."

A bread roll bounces past my feet, leaving a trail of breadcrumbs in its wake. I laugh at the absurdity of it all. "Should we try to catch the food?" I ask, eyeing a plate of green beans slithering across the grass like a snake.

She shakes her head, wearing a rueful grin. "That might make things worse. Let's just enjoy the show, shall we? It'll wear off...eventually."

As if on cue, a turkey, still on its platter, stands up on its baked legs and begins to strut around, somewhat muffled-gobbling indignantly. Guests scramble out of its way, equal parts amused and alarmed.

I spot Ronan across the glen, trying to wrangle a group of escaping dinner rolls. Our gazes meet, and he grins, shrugging as if to say, "Just another day in Evershift Haven."

A chorus of shrieks draws my attention. A massive gelatin mold has come to life, resembling a gelatinous blob monster from a B-movie. It oozes its way down the buffet table, absorbing smaller dishes in its path.

"Oh, dear," murmurs Grizelda beside me. "That wasn't supposed to happen."

I turn to her, unable to keep the laughter from my voice. "What exactly was supposed to happen?"

She pats her belly absentmindedly. "I was trying to expand the portions. You know, a little magical boost to our Thanksgiving feast. I didn't expect it to become quite so lively," she says to Atlas, who puts a massive around her back, settling on the curve of her waist. "It's mostly your fault, since you made me pregnant, and that messes with my magic." Her eyes twinkle as she says that.

He laughs, and it sounds like two boulders rubbing together. "I'll take the blame for that."

A cranberry sauce rocket whizzes past, leaving a trail of red splatters in its wake. I duck, narrowly avoiding a facial. "I can see that," I say, wiping a stray cranberry from my cheek. "How long until this wears off?"

She purses her lips, considering. "Oh, an hour or two. Maybe three. Possibly by dessert?"

I shake my head, amazed at how calmly she's taking all this, but then again, in a town where magic is an everyday occurrence, maybe animated food isn't that unusual.

"So," I say, brushing off my clothes, "I guess we should try to make the best of it. Any ideas on how to have Thanksgiving dinner when the dinner is trying to escape?"

She grins. "Oh, I know just the thing. We'll turn it into a game. Whoever catches the most food gets an extra slice of pumpkin pie...once we manage to ground those flying ones, of course."

As if in response, a pumpkin pie swoops low, narrowly missing Grizelda's head. She ducks, laughing. "See? They're already playing along."

I survey the chaotic scene unfolding before me, amusement and disbelief washing over me. The once-orderly Thanksgiving feast has transformed into a surreal battlefield of animated food.

Ronan catches my eye from across the glen with bewilderment and mirth. "Candice." he calls out, dodging a flying dinner roll. "We need to contain this before it gets out of hand."

I nod, agreeing despite Grizelda's plan to let it run its course. I scan the area for anything that might help and see a stack of empty baskets near the edge of the clearing. "The baskets. Maybe we can use them to catch the smaller dishes?"

He gives me a thumbs up and starts making his way toward the baskets, weaving through the chaos like a dancer avoiding his partner's toes. I follow suit, ducking under a low-flying pumpkin pie.

When we reach the baskets, a group of townspeople joins us, led by Throk. The orc's green skin is splattered with various food stains, giving him a comical appearance.

"Good thinking," he says, grabbing a basket. "Let's round up these culinary troublemakers."

We spread out, baskets in hand, and attempt to capture the runaway dishes. I'm chasing after a group of escaping dinner rolls, their little bread bodies bouncing along the grass. "Come here, you little carb monsters," I mutter, lunging forward with my basket. I manage to scoop up three of them, but the fourth takes an unexpected turn, evading my grasp.

Nearby, Ronan is locked in an epic showdown with the runaway roasted turkey that should've been the star of the feast, if it hadn't decided to go rogue. The bird, perfectly cooked to a golden brown and larger than a wheelbarrow, struts around with impressive indignation, managing a fierce sort of gobble despite its lack of a head. It weaves through tables, its gleaming skin catching the sunlight, looking very much like it knows it's supposed to be eaten but has absolutely no intention of letting that happen.

Ronan holds a large basket in front of him like he's taming a wild beast. "Easy there, big fella," he says, inching closer with exaggerated care. "How about we call a truce? You stop charging, and I promise not to eat you."

The turkey seems to consider this, tilting slightly as though it can still see him, even without eyes. Its wings twitch, dripping buttery goodness as it nearly bristles with outrage, and it puffs up, letting out a defiant, garbled "Gobble."—an impressive feat for a bird with no head. Then, in a display of pure Thanksgiving spirit, it charges at him with all the ferocity of a small, flightless bull.

Ronan's pupils dilate as he dives to the side, narrowly missing a collision with the bird's impressive bulk. He lands face-first in a massive pile of mashed potatoes, disappearing momentarily in a cloud of buttery fluff before emerging with a startled, disgruntled expression. The lycan pulls himself up, dripping in creamy potatoes, with stray parsley flakes sticking to his fur.

The sight sends me into a fit of laughter I can't quite suppress. "Ronan," I say between giggles, "I think he might have won that round."

With a slow, defeated grin spreading across his face, he shakes some mashed potatoes off his hand. "Think this is funny, do you?" he asks, scooping up a handful of mashed potatoes.

I back away, holding up my hands in mock surrender. "Let's not do anything rash—"

But it's too late. The glob of mashed potatoes flies through the air, hitting me square in the chest. I gasp, looking down at the mess on my shirt, then back up at his mischievous grin.

"Oh, it's on," I declare, reaching for the nearest food item—a bowl of cranberry sauce and chucking it toward him. Most of it flies out, but a gob lands on his muzzle, and he licks it off.

Grizelda stands in the middle of it all, her wild hair now adorned with bits of stuffing and gravy. She throws back her head, laughing uproariously. "This isn't quite what I had in mind, but it certainly is festive."

I duck behind a table, using it as cover as I prepare my next attack. Ronan appears beside me, his fur now a rainbow of food stains.

"Having fun yet?" he asks with amusement.

I grin, wiping a smear of gravy from my cheek. "You know what? I actually am. This is the craziest Thanksgiving I've ever had."

"Well, then," he says, scooping up a handful of stuffing, "Let's make it even crazier." He pops up from behind the table, lobbing the stuffing at Throk. The orc turns just in time to get a faceful of herbed bread cubes. He sputters, wiping his eyes, then grins menacingly.

"You'll pay for that, pup." Throk snatches a whole pumpkin pie from midair.

I peek over the edge of the table as Throk winds up for his throw. "Ronan, incoming."

He ducks, and the pie sails over his head—right into the face of a startled elf, who had just rounded the corner of a nearby booth. The elf stands there for a moment, pie tin sliding down his face to reveal eyes blinking in shock through a mask of pumpkin filling.

For a moment, everything goes quiet. Then the elf's face splits into a wide grin, and he grabs a bowl of green bean casserole. "Food fight," he yells, flinging the casserole into the crowd.

Before I know it, the containment effort has devolved into a full-blown food fight. Townspeople are lobbing yams at each other, dodging airborne pies, and using serving trays as shields against the onslaught of flying food. I grab a ladle of gravy, flinging it in a wide arc. It splatters across several people, including a fairy whose wings are now coated in the savory sauce.

"Sorry," I call out, but the fairy just laughs, shaking her wings and sending droplets of gravy flying everywhere.

Ronan grabs my hand, pulling me out from behind the table. "Let's get to higher ground."

We make our way to a small hill overlooking the glen, dodging flying food as we go. From our vantage point, we can see the full extent of the chaos below. The once-pristine clearing is now a patchwork of food splatters, with people running, laughing, and flinging edible projectiles in every direction as the animated food still tries to slink off.

I lean against Ronan while we catch our breath. "When I imagined my first Thanksgiving in Evershift Haven, this isn't quite what I had in mind."

He chuckles while wrapping an arm around my shoulders. "Welcome to Evershift Haven, where even our holidays are magical—and sometimes a little messy."

Watching the food fight continue below, I'm filled with warmth that has nothing to do with the exertion of the battle. This quirky, magical town and its inhabitants have welcomed me with open arms—and apparently, open plates.

A glob of mashed sweet potatoes sails past us, missing us by inches. Ronan and I exchange a look, then grab handfuls of the orange mush.

"Ready for round two?" he asks, a playful glint in his eye.

I nod, grinning from ear to ear. "Absolutely. Let's show them how it's done."

Hand in hand, we charge back down the hill, armed with our sweet potato ammunition, ready to rejoin the fray. As I fling my handful of mash at an unsuspecting dryad, I realize this might just be the best Thanksgiving I've ever had.

The food fight rages on. A squadron of dinner rolls zooms overhead like tiny, doughy fighter jets, dropping payload of butter pats on unsuspecting revelers below. The giant gelatin mold blob monster oozes its way through the crowd, absorbing smaller food items and growing larger by the minute.

"Watch out for the Jell-O Beast," yells someone, and people scatter as it approaches, leaving trails of sticky residue in its wake.

I grab Ronan's arm, pointing at the wobbling monstrosity. "We need to stop that thing before it consumes the whole feast."

"I've got an idea. Follow me."

He leads me to a table laden with pies—the few that haven't yet taken flight. "We'll build a pie barricade," he says, grabbing an armful of the desserts. "The Jell-O Beast won't be able to absorb these as easily."

I catch on quickly, gathering my own stack of pies. We work together, creating a circular wall of pies around the approaching jello monster. As it reaches our dessert fortification, it pauses, quivering, as if confused.

"It's working." I say, watching as the Jello Beast tries to absorb a cherry pie, only to find its gelatinous body repelled by the flaky crust.

Our success is short-lived, however, as the turkey—still very much alive and now sporting a gravy-slicked coat—charges through our pie barricade, scattering desserts everywhere. The Jell-O Beast seizes the opportunity, oozing through the gap and continuing its relentless advance.

"That didn't go as intended," he says, wiping cherry filling from his fur.

I laugh at the absurdity of it all. "I guess we'll have to think of something else. Any other bright ideas?"

Before Ronan can respond, Grizelda's voice booms across the glen, magically amplified to be heard over the chaos. "Attention, everyone. I think I've figured out how to end this little...mishap."

All gazes turn to the town witch, who stands atop a table, her hair now resembling a bird's nest filled with various food items. She raises her arms, fingers sparkling with magical energy.

"On the count of three," she calls out, "Everyone grab the nearest enchanted food item so we can share the magic of the town. Ready? One... two... three."

As she brings her arms down in a sweeping motion, I lunge for a levitating bowl of cranberry sauce. All around me, people are grappling with animated dishes, pies, and various other foodstuffs. The air fills with a tingling energy, and for a moment, everything seems to freeze. Ronan manages to grab the turkey.

Then, as suddenly as it began, the chaos subsides. The bowl of cranberry sauce in my hands stops trying to escape, settling into a normal, inanimate state. All around the glen, people are holding now-ordinary dishes of food, looking both relieved and slightly disappointed that the excitement is over. Ronan is holding the huge turkey, still enlarged but now inanimate, and lets out an "oomph," as he staggers under the sudden dead weight.

Chapter 8

I STAND TRANSFIXED as Grizelda keeps her hands raised. The chaotic scene around us falls silent, with everyone holding their breath. Her reputation for magical mishaps might worry some of the others, but there's a confidence in her stance that gives me hope.

"Don't worry, darlings." Grizelda winks. "I've got this under control."

She begins to murmur words too low for me to catch. A soft, shimmering glow emanates from her fingertips, spreading outward to fill the entire square. The light dances all of us as the food returns to the table. Some dishes, like the turkey, remain enlarged, but others have reverted to normal or missed the effects of the haywire spell entirely.

Grizelda snaps her fingers with a flourish. A soft shimmer passes over the assembled crowd, and the food splatters adorning my clothes and hair vanish without a trace. Around me, others pat themselves down in disbelief, finding themselves suddenly clean and presentable.

The tables and chairs right themselves, tablecloths smoothing out as if by invisible hands. Centerpieces reappear, perfectly arranged. Even the grass beneath our feet, trampled during the food fight, springs back to life, looking freshly manicured.

As the last remnants of the chaos settle, a collective sigh of relief ripples through the crowd. Then, as if on cue, cheers and applause erupt. Grizelda takes a small, proud bow, her wild purple hair bouncing with the movement.

"That was incredible," I whisper, still in awe of what I've just witnessed.

Ronan grins beside me. "Grizelda may cause her fair share of magical mishaps, but when it counts, she always comes through."

Mayor Ambrosius steps forward, his long white beard still slightly stained with cranberry sauce. "Thank you, Grizelda. Your quick thinking has saved our celebration."

She waves a hand dismissively. "Oh, it was nothing. Just a little magical tidying up. Now, shall we eat? I don't know about you all, but that food fight has left me famished."

Laughter ripples through the crowd as people begin to make their way back to the tables. I hang back, still processing everything that's happened. Ronan touches my arm.

"You okay?" he asks. "I know this is a lot to take in."

I nod slowly. "It's just... I've never seen anything like that before. In my world, magic is just tricks and illusions, but this was real."

Ronan smiles softly. "Welcome to Evershift Haven, where the impossible is just another Tuesday...or Friday," he adds with a wink, alluding to the postponement of the feast due to yesterday's weather.

Making our way to a table, Grizelda approaches us. Up close, I can see the faint sheen of sweat on her pale-green ski,n and the slight tremor in her hands—signs of the effort her spell required.

"Candice, dear," she says warmly. "I hope our little magical mishap didn't scare you off. How are you finding Evershift Haven so far?"

I laugh, a bit nervously. "It's certainly never dull. That was amazing, what you did. Thank you for saving the feast." I don't bother pointing out she was the one who derailed it to start with.

Grizelda beams. "Oh, it's all in a day's work for the town witch. Now, tell me, have you tried the pumpkin pie yet? I infused it with a little happiness spell—guaranteed to bring a smile to your face."

As she chatters on about her magical dessert, I'm amazed at how quickly the extraordinary has become ordinary here. Just days ago, I would have dismissed talk of happiness spells and magical mishaps as fantasy or insanity. Now, I'm eagerly anticipating a slice of enchanted pumpkin pie.

"You simply must try the cranberry sauce," she insists. "Caelan infused it with a touch of joy. One bite, and you'll be grinning from ear to ear."

I nod, still processing the idea of emotion-infused food. "That sounds... interesting. Is it safe?"

"Oh, perfectly safe, dear. Just a smidge of magic to enhance the flavors and lift the spirits. Nothing too potent."

Ronan chuckles beside me. "Don't worry, Candice. Caelan's food magic is harmless, though I'd steer clear of his giggle-inducing gravy if I were you. Last year, half the town couldn't stop laughing for hours."

The witch chuckles. "That was one time. Caelan assured me he's perfected the recipe since then."

As we make our way to the tables, I'm struck by the vibrant array of dishes spread before us. Turkeys with golden, crackling skin sit alongside colorful vegetable platters that seem to shimmer in the light. Pies of every variety line the dessert table, their aromas mingling in the crisp autumn air. It's truly like the food fight never happened.

Ronan guides me to a seat. We settle in next to Suzette and Throk, who are already engaged in animated conversation.

"Did you see Grizelda's save earlier?" asks Throk, his deep voice rumbling with amusement. "I thought for sure we'd be chasing that gelatinous menace all the way to the Whispering Woods."

Suzette laughs, sounding carefree. It's a total contrast to the stressed-out sister I remember from before she discovered Evershift Haven. "I'm just glad she managed to stop it before it reached 'Mystical Motors.' Can you imagine trying to get gelatin monster out of an engine?"

I giggle at the mental image. "Is this normal for Evershift Haven? Magical food fights and dancing decorations?"

Throk grins, his tusks glinting in the sunlight. "Normal? Not exactly, but it's not exactly out of the ordinary either. Life here is always an adventure."

As we begin to fill our plates, I'm amazed by the variety of dishes. Alongside traditional Thanksgiving fare, there are foods I've never seen before—a shimmering blue gelatin that seems to change flavors with each bite, bread rolls that float just above the basket, and a gravy boat that refills itself.

"This is incredible," I say, taking a bite of mashed potatoes that taste like they were made from clouds. "I've never experienced anything like this."

Ronan beams, clearly pleased by my enthusiasm. "Wait until you try the stuffing. It's my mother's recipe, passed down through generations of lycans. She taught it to Caelan when she was his sous chef years ago."

I raise an eyebrow. "Lycan stuffing? Should I be worried?"

He laughs, a rich, warm sound that sends a pleasant shiver down my spine. "No need to worry. It's made with herbs from the Whispering Woods. The trees themselves recommend the best combinations each year."

As we eat, conversation flows easily. Stories of past Thanksgivings in Evershift Haven are shared, each more fantastical than the last. I learn about the year a flock of enchanted turkeys crashed the festivities, demanding to be guests rather than the main course, and the time when a miscalculation in Grizelda's enlargement spell resulted in a pumpkin pie the size of a house. They had leftovers until almost Christmas Eve.

Throughout the meal, Ronan watches me. Each time our gazes meet, I'm reminded of our night together, and of the connection that seems to be growing stronger with each passing moment.

As the meal winds down, Suzette tilts her head my way, indicating she wants to talk privately. I excuse myself from the table and follow her to a quiet corner of the square.

"So," she says, a knowing smile on her face. "Did you have a good night last night?"

My cheeks flush, but I smile. "I did. We got caught in the storm, and..." I waggle my eyebrows to her appreciative giggle.

Her expression turns thoughtful. "Are you planning to return to Chicago next week?"

I hesitate, suddenly realizing I haven't given much thought to my departure. The idea of leaving Evershift Haven, and Ronan, creates an unexpected ache in my chest. "I'm...not sure yet," I confess.

Suzette squeezes my hand in a silent show of support. "There's no rush to decide. Evershift Haven has a way of helping people find their place, even if they didn't know they were looking for one."

I nod. "It's just...everything here is so different, and so magical. Part of me can't imagine going back to my old life, but another part is terrified of such a big change."

Her expression softens. "I get it. I felt the same way when I first arrived, but I've never seen you look as happy or as alive as you do right now. Maybe that's worth exploring?"

Before I can respond, Ronan appear beside us. "Everything okay?" he asks with concern.

I nod, offering him a reassuring smile. "Everything's fine. Suzette and I were just catching up."

She gives my hand one last squeeze and opens her mouth to say more, but Mayor Ambrosius's voice booms across the square, calling everyone to attention.

"Friends, neighbors, and honored guests," he says, his long white beard now impeccably groomed. "We gather today to celebrate not only the bounty of our harvest but the spirit of community that makes Evershift Haven so special."

As the mayor continues his speech, I can't look away from Ronan. He stands tall and proud, his powerful frame a stark contrast to the delicate china he's carefully arranging as we pitch in to help with the quiet transition from savory to sweet during the speech. When he catches me looking, he winks, sending a thrill through me.

When the speech ends, the dessert buffet begins in earnest, and I'm swept up in a whirlwind of flavors, laughter, and conversation. As I take my first bite of Grizelda's pumpkin pie, a wave of pure joy washes over me. It's not overwhelming or artificial, but a gentle warmth that spreads from my chest to the tips of my fingers and toes. I look up, catching her gaze across the table. She gives me a knowing smile and a thumbs-up.

"Good, isn't it?" asks Ronan, leaning close. His breath tickles my ear.

"It's incredible," I say, offering him a forkful. "Here, try some."

He opens his mouth, allowing me to feed him the bite of pie. As he savors it, his eyelids close in bliss, and I'm struck by how natural this feels—sharing food, sharing joy, and sharing a moment of quiet intimacy amid the bustling celebration.

As the evening wears on, I'm drawn into conversations with various townsfolk. Each has a story to tell, or a bit of magic to share. Puckley shares tales of talking vegetables and mischievous weeds. Bella from "The Enchanted Espresso" demonstrates her ability to create latte art that moves and changes based on the drinker's mood.

Through it all, Ronan remains at my side. He fills in gaps in my knowledge, introduces me to people I haven't met, and keeps my glass full. His attentiveness warms me more than any magical brew ever could.

As the sun begins to set, casting a golden glow over the square, Throk stands and raises his glass. "A toast," he calls out, his deep voice carrying easily over the chatter. "To new friends and old, to the magic that binds us, and to the love that sustains us."

"Hear, hear," echoes the crowd before glasses clink all around.

I raise my own glass, meeting Ronan's gaze over the rim. Surrounded by the warmth and wonder of Evershift Haven, I realize I'm facing a choice. The life I've known in Chicago seems a world away, while this new reality—full of magic, adventure, and the promise of something deeper with Ronan—beckons enticingly.

As the feast winds down, I'm caught in a whirlwind of emotions. The magic of Evershift Haven surrounds me, from the twinkling lights that dance in the air to the laughter that seems to shimmer with its own enchantment. I'm lost in thought when his gentle touch on my arm brings me back to the present.

He smiles at me. "Care for a walk?"

My heart beats erratically. There's something in his tone, a hint of significance that makes me suspect this isn't just a casual stroll. I nod, unable to find my voice for a moment.

We slip away from the crowd, and I notice the enchanted cornucopia still glowing steadily at the center of the feast table. Its warm light seems to follow us. The evening air is crisp with the scent of fallen leaves and distant bonfires.

We walk in companionable silence for a while, our footsteps crunching on the leaf-strewn path. The town square gradually fades behind us, replaced by the peaceful whisper of trees. I sneak glances at Ronan, admiring how the moonlight plays across his strong features, and the way his fur seems to absorb the shadows.

"That was some feast, huh?" I say.

He chuckles. "I could have done without the animated turkey incident."

I laugh, remembering the chaos. "I don't know. I thought it added a certain...excitement to the evening."

"Is that what we're calling near-death by poultry these days?"

We share a laugh, and I move closer to him, drawn by his warmth in the cool night air.

"Candice," he says, his tone turning serious. He stops walking and turns to face me. "I wanted to talk to you about something."

My breath catches in my throat. *Here it comes*, I think. The conversation I've been both anticipating and dreading.

"I know you're planning to go back to Chicago soon," he says, looking pained. "I respect that. Your life is there, your job, your friends, but I can't help wondering...is there a chance you might consider staying in Evershift Haven?"

Chapter 9

RONAN'S WORDS HANG in the air while he looks at me intently. I draw in a deep breath of the cool evening air. "When I first arrived here, I thought I'd lost my mind. Everything seemed impossible, like a dream I couldn't wake up from, but now..." I pause, gesturing to the magical town around us. "I feel more awake than I ever have before."

His ears perk up as a hopeful expression crosses his face.

I continue. "I've never been more at home anywhere in my life. The magic, the community, and the way everyone embraces who they truly are—it's everything I never knew I was missing."

His tail starts to wag slightly, and I smile at his enthusiasm. "And the farming, Ronan. Working with these magical plants and coaxing life from the earth in ways I never imagined possible—just the idea has awakened a passion I didn't know I had."

"Really?" he asks, his voice filled with excitement. "You're considering staying?"

I nod, an invisible weight lift from my shoulders as I make the decision. "More than considering. I want to stay. I want to build a life here, to see what I can create with my own two hands and a little bit of magic."

His muzzle splits into a wide grin. "That's wonderful. I promise I'll support you every step of the way. In fact..." He pauses, suddenly looking a bit nervous. "I have some land, just on the outskirts of town. I briefly mentioned it before... It's been in my family for generations, but I've never quite known what to do with it. If you'd like, it could be the perfect place for you to start your farm."

My eyes widen. "Are you serious? That's incredibly generous."

He shrugs, a bashful look crossing his face. "It's nothing, really. The land deserves to be used by someone who'll love it, and I think you're just the person to bring it to life."

Overwhelmed with emotion, I throw my arms around him, burying my face in his furry chest. His strong arms encircle me, and I feel safe and like I've finally found where I belong.

We sit down on a nearby bench, our bodies close, and the warmth of his fur is a welcome buffer against the cool air. We start to discuss our vision for the future, and I'm struck by how natural it feels, and how easily our lives seem to intertwine.

"Tell me about this land of yours," I say, eager to hear more.

"It's beautiful. About ten acres, with open fields and wooded areas. There's a small stream running through it, fed by an underground spring. The soil is rich—my grandmother used to say it was blessed by the earth spirits themselves."

I listen, enraptured, as he paints a picture of the land in my mind. I can almost see the fields stretching out before me, feel the cool water of the stream, and smell the rich earth beneath my feet.

"What would you want to grow?" he asks, his tail swishing with excitement.

I ponder for a moment, remembering all I've learned about magical farming in my short time here. "I'd love to start with some of the basics—those singing sunflowers we saw at Puckley's farm, and maybe some whispering wheat. Oh, and definitely a pumpkin patch."

Ronan nods. "Those are great ideas, and don't forget, we could plant some moon-blooming night lilies along the stream. They're not only beautiful, but their petals are used in all sorts of magical remedies."

As we continue to plan, the ideas flow freely between us. We discuss crop rotations, magical pest control methods, and even the possibility of raising some mystical livestock. With each passing moment, our shared vision becomes clearer.

Still talking, and hand in hand, we meander back to the feast. The autumn air now smells like spiced cider and roasted chestnuts, mingling with the faint aroma of ozone from the magic that permeates Evershift Haven.

As we approach, Grizelda beams at our intertwined fingers. "Looks like someone's made a decision."

I blush, acutely aware of Ronan's warm, furry hand in mine. "I have," I say, unable to keep the smile from my face. "I'm staying in Evershift Haven."

Grizelda turns to her husband. "Five bucks. I told you she'd stay."

Atlas looks puzzled. "I don't recall betting otherwise, love."

She frowns at him for a moment but sighs. "No, I guess you didn't." Then she spins back to face me. "It's truly marvelous. We must get you settled then. As the guardian witch of Evershift Haven, one of my duties is creating housing. I have just the thing—how about a charming mushroom cottage? Or perhaps a cozy pumpkin house? I can whip one up in no time with a flick of my wrist."

Before I can respond, Ronan says, "Actually, Grizelda, I had a different idea." He turns to me. "Candi, you could stay with me. We can build your dream farm right there on my family's land." He glances at Grizelda. "We might need to move my cabin there though."

That seems to mollify the witch, but I'm still processing the idea. The thought of creating a home and a farm with Ronan fills me with an excitement I've never known before. "Really? You'd want that?"

Ronan nods, his furry ears twitching slightly. "More than anything."

"Then, yes," I say, squeezing his hand. "Yes, I'd love that."

Grizelda's grin widens, and she winks at us. "Ah, young love. It's a magic all its own, you know."

Suddenly, Puckley emerges from the crowd, her moss-covered skin practically glowing with enthusiasm. "Did I hear correctly? Our Candice is staying and starting a farm?"

I nod, still barely believing it myself. "That's right. Ronan's offered his family's land."

Puckley looks delighted, and the tiny flowers in her hair seem to bloom even brighter. "Oh, how wonderful. I'd be more than happy to mentor you in magical farming. There's so much to learn—talking to plants, coaxing stubborn seeds to grow, negotiating with the seasons..."

"I'd love that, Puckley," I say, genuinely touched by her offer. "I have so much to learn."

As the reality of my decision sinks in, a new thought occurs to me. I turn to Ronan, suddenly nervous. "Do you think...would it be okay if I invited my best friend, Evony, to visit for Christmas? I'd love for her to see all this magic."

He nods. "Of course. This is your home now too. Your friends are welcome here."

Overwhelmed with gratitude and excitement, I spot Suzette across the glade. "Excuse me for a moment," I say before making my way through the crowd.

Suzette is chatting with a group of elves, her lawyer's poise slightly at odds with the fantastical surroundings. When she sees me approach, she excuses herself and meets me halfway. "Hey, sis," she says, searching my face. "You look...different. Happy."

I nod, hardly able to contain my news. "I've decided to stay in Evershift Haven."

She grins. "I had a feeling you might. This place has a way of getting under your skin, doesn't it?"

I nod. "It really does, and there's more—Ronan's offered to let me start a farm on his family's land. We're going to build a life here together."

She gives me a wide grin. "Oh, Candice, that's wonderful. I'm so happy for you."

"Thanks, Suz," I say, pulling her into a hug. As we embrace, I ask, "What do you think about inviting Evony for Christmas? I'd love for her to experience the magic of Evershift Haven too."

She pulls back, her eyes sparkling with excitement. "That's a brilliant idea. Evony's always had a secret soft spot for fantasy. I bet she'd love it here."

As we stand there, I'm struck by how much my life has changed in such a short time. From a vaguely dissatisfied event planner to a soon-to-be magical farmer, it's been quite the journey, and as I look around at the fantastical beings that now feel like family, it's only just beginning.

Ronan approaches, his tall frame easily visible above the crowd. He wraps an arm around my waist, and I lean into him, savoring his warmth and strength.

"Did you tell your sister our news?"

I nod, excitement bubbling up inside me. "Absolutely, and I think we need to celebrate. After all, it's not every day a girl decides to stay in a magical town and start a new life with a sexy lycan."

He grins. "I couldn't agree more. What do you say we grab some of Caelan's flambé fae fruit with hot cider and find a quiet spot to watch the enchanted fireworks?"

I nod, and we make our way through the feast, hand in hand. Passing Grizelda, she gives me another knowing wink and waves her hand. Suddenly, a shower of golden sparks rains down around us, each one transforming into a tiny, glowing butterfly before disappearing.

"Welcome home, Candice," she calls out, her voice carrying over the festive noise.

Home.

Surrounded by magic, love, and endless possibilities, I've truly found where I belong.

About Aurelia

AURELIA SKYE IS THE pen name *USA Today* bestselling author Kit Tunstall uses when writing science fiction and paranormal romance, along with paranormal women's fiction. It's simply a way to separate the myriad types of stories she writes so readers know what to expect with each "author."

If you enjoyed this story and would like to receive notifications of new releases or access bonus chapters for your favorite books, please join my Mailing List[1]. You'll also receive free books just for joining. If you prefer to receive notifications for just one, or a few, of my pen names, you'll have the option to select which lists to subscribe to at signup.

1.　http://kittunstall.com/newsletter/

Also by Aurelia Skye

Alien Baby Pact
Baby For The Brundle Commander
Baby For The Serp General
Alien Baby Pact Compilation
Baby For The Grimlock General
Baby For The Palantir Chief
Baby For The Alphan Captain
Baby For The Mosaic Med Chief
Baby For The Tark Commander

Alien Baby Pakt
Alien Baby Pakt Zusammenstellung

BioCircuit Nexus
Cyborgs' Origins
Cyborg's Tether

Celestial Mates
Wrong Place, Right Mate
Destined For The Drakari Warlords

Cybernetic Hearts
Mated To The Cyborg General
Claimed By The Cyborg Commander
Fated For The Cyborg Officer
Meant For The Cyborg Captain
Baby For The Cyborg General
Cybernetic Hearts: Complete Series
Cœurs Cybernétiques: Série Complète

Dazon Agenda
Written In The Stars
Alien's Babies
Diplomatic Affairs
Moon Madness
Across The Stars
Emperor's Assassin Bride
Dazon Agenda: Complete Collection
Compilation de l'Agenda Dazon

Evershift Haven
Pumpkin Spice and Orc's Delight
Howls & Harvest

Future Fairytales
Hooked

Guerriers Blessés

Chassé
Inlassable
Marqué
Justice
Compilation Guerriers Blessés

Harrow Bay
Hell Gates & Hot Flashes
Nightmares & Night Sweats
Warlocks & Wrinkles
Love Spells & Liver Spots
Phantasms & Presbyopia
Vampires & Varicose Veins
Mermaids & Mood Swings
Séances & Sagging Skin
Necromancy & Knee Pains
Marids & Memory Loss
Devil Deals & Dizzy Spells
Happy Endings & New Beginnings
Harrow Bay, Volume 1
Hellhounds & Mistletoe
Harrow Bay, Volume 2
Harrow Bay, Volume 3
Harrow Bay Complete Series

Harrow Bucht Serie
Höllentore & Hitzewallungen
Alpträume Und Nachtschweiß
Hexenmeister & Falten
Liebeszauber Und Leberflecken
Phantasmen Und Alterssichtigkeit
Vampire und Krampfadern

Meerjungfrauen Und Stimmungsschwankungen
Séancen Und Schlaffe Haut
Nekromantie Und Knieschmerzen
Marids und Gedächtnisverlust
Teufelsgeschäfte Und Schwindelzauber
Happy Ends Und Neuanfängen
Höllenhunde & Mistelzweige

Hell Virus
Catching Hell
Surviving Hell
Bleeding Hell
Raising Hell
Sharing Hell

Howls Romance
The Jaguar Alpha's Forbidden Lover
CEO Wolf Shifter's Surprise Twins

Northstar Shifters
Northstar Heir's Scarred Mate

Olympus Station
Station Commander's Surrogate
Alien Prince's Secret Baby
Security Agent's Alien Bartender
Olympus Station Compilation

SpicyShorts
Music In My Heart
Kilted Tentacle Monster: A Search for True Love

Sweet Escapes
Hook & Wendy

The Haunting of Clara Gray
Ghostly Awakening
Ghostly Harmonies

Three Crones Inn
Vastly Inn-proved
Ghastly Intentions
Grave Inn-tervention
Ghostly Inn-heritance
Three Crones Inn Compilation

True North
True North #1: Death & Deception
True North #2: Rescued & Revelations
True North #3: Fire & Ice
True North #4: Enemies & Lovers
True North #5: Truth & Tiranog
True North #6: Fight & Flight
True North #7: Love & Loss

Wounded Warriors
Relentless
Marked
Justice
Wounded Warriors Collection
Hunted

Standalone
Reluctant Companion
Princess By Mistake
Fire Lord's Assistant
True North
Dragon Laird's Witch
Alien General's Rebel Consort
Tempted By Demons
Enemy Combatant
Grotesquerie
Mistaken Bounty
Wahre Richtung
Power Surges & Amorous Urges
Taken By The Orc General
Compilation Alien Baby Pact

Also by Kit Tunstall

After The End
Unraveling
Unyielding

Cybernetic Hearts
Cœurs Cybernétiques: Série Complète

Evershift Haven
Howls & Harvest

Howls Romance
CEO Wolf Shifter's Surprise Twins

TnT Storybuilders
Building Your World: A Guide For Writers
Action Thriller Storybuilder: A Guide For Writers
Instant Love Novelette Storybuilder
Instant Love Novella Storybuilder: A Guide For Writers
Contemporary Reverse Harem Novel Storybuilder

Contemporary Romance Novel Storybuilder
Cozy Mystery Novel Storybuilder
Dark Romance Storybuilder
Gothic Romance Storybuilder
Ménage Novelette Storybuilder
Ménage Novella Storybuilder
Ménage Novel Storybuilder
Paranormal Revere Harem Storybuilder
Paranormal Romance Novel Storybuilder
Psychological Thriller Storybuilder
Regency Romance Storybuilder
Science Fiction Romance Novella Storybuilder
Spicy Novella Storybuilder
Sweet Novella Storybuilder
Romantic Suspense Storybuilder: A Guide For Writers
Postapocalyptic Thriller Trilogy Storybuilder
Horror Novel Storybuilder

Standalone
Holiday Tales: Four Short Stories of Thanksgiving and Christmas
Master's Gift
Dragon Laird's Witch
Baby Daddies: Older Men & Babies Collection
Christmas Kiss: Limited Edition Six-Story Holiday Collection
Sampler: SF, Contemporary & Historical Collection

Watch for more at www.kittunstall.com.

www.ingramcontent.com/pod-product-compliance
Lightning Source LLC
Chambersburg PA
CBHW061348140726
47997CB00003B/1102